A RIVER RUNS THROUGH IT

Norman Maclean

A RIVER RUNS
THROUGH IT

Wood engravings by Barry Moser

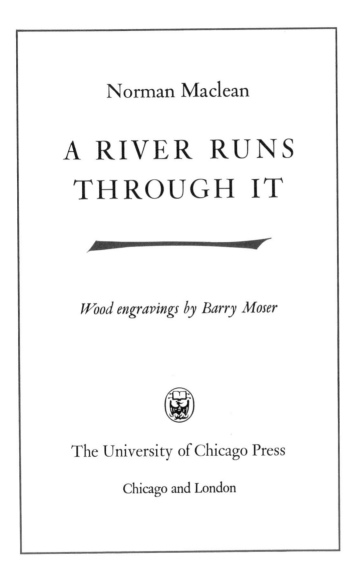

The University of Chicago Press

Chicago and London

A River Runs Through It originally appeared as the first of three
stories by Norman Maclean, published together as *A River Runs
Through It and Other Stories* (University of Chicago Press, 1976).

The University of Chicago Press, Chicago 60637
The University of Chicago Press, Ltd., London

Printed in the United States of America

01 00 99 98 97 96 95 94 93   8 9 10

LIBRARY OF CONGRESS CATALOGING-IN-PUBLICATION DATA

Maclean, Norman, 1902–
    A river runs through it / Norman Maclean ; designed and
illustrated by Barry Moser.
        p. cm.
    Originally appeared as the first of three stories, published
together as A river runs through it, and other stories. 1976.
    ISBN 0–226–50060–8 (alk. paper)
    I. Moser, Barry. II. Title.
PS3563.A317993R58 1989   88–38576
813'.54—dc19   CIP

For Jean and John
to whom I have long told stories

*I*N OUR FAMILY, there was no clear line between religion and fly fishing. We lived at the junction of great trout rivers in western Montana, and our father was a Presbyterian minister and a fly fisherman who tied his own flies and taught others. He told us about Christ's disciples being fishermen, and we were left to assume, as my brother and I did, that all first-class fishermen on the Sea of Galilee were fly fishermen and that John, the favorite, was a dry-fly fisherman.

It is true that one day a week was given over wholly to religion. On Sunday mornings my brother, Paul, and I went to Sunday school and then to "morning services" to hear our father preach and in the evenings to Christian

Endeavor and afterwards to "evening services" to hear our father preach again. In between on Sunday afternoons we had to study *The Westminster Shorter Catechism* for an hour and then recite before we could walk the hills with him while he unwound between services. But he never asked us more than the first question in the catechism, "What is the chief end of man?" And we answered together so one of us could carry on if the other forgot, "Man's chief end is to glorify God, and to enjoy Him forever." This always seemed to satisfy him, as indeed such a beautiful answer should have, and besides he was anxious to be on the hills where he could restore his soul and be filled again to overflowing for the evening sermon. His chief way of recharging himself was to recite to us from the sermon that was coming, enriched here and there with selections from the most successful passages of his morning sermon.

Even so, in a typical week of our childhood Paul and I probably received as many hours of instruction in fly fishing as we did in all other spiritual matters.

After my brother and I became good fishermen, we realized that our father was not a great fly caster, but he was accurate and stylish and wore a glove on his casting hand. As he buttoned his glove in preparation to giving us a lesson, he would say, "It is an art that is performed on a four-count rhythm between ten and two o'clock."

As a Scot and a Presbyterian, my father believed that man by nature was a mess and had fallen from an original state of grace. Somehow, I early developed the notion that he had done this by falling from a tree. As for my father, I never knew whether he believed God was a mathematician but he certainly believed God could count and that only by picking up God's rhythms were we able to regain power and beauty. Unlike many Presbyterians, he often used the word "beautiful."

After he buttoned his glove, he would hold his rod straight out in front of him, where it trembled with the beating of his heart. Although it was eight and a half feet long, it weighed only four and a half ounces. It was made of split bamboo cane from the far-off Bay of Tonkin. It was wrapped with red and blue silk thread, and the wrappings were carefully spaced to make the delicate rod powerful but not so stiff it could not tremble.

Always it was to be called a rod. If someone called it a pole, my father looked at him as a sergeant in the United States Marines would look at a recruit who had just called a rifle a gun.

My brother and I would have preferred to start learning how to fish by going out and catching a few, omitting entirely anything difficult or technical in the way of preparation that would take away from the fun. But it wasn't by way of fun that we were introduced to our father's art. If our father had had his say, nobody who did not know how to fish would be allowed to disgrace a fish by catching him. So you too will have to approach the art Marine- and Presbyterian-style, and, if you have never picked up a fly rod before, you will soon find it factually and theologically true that man by nature is a damn mess. The four-and-a-half-ounce thing in silk wrappings that trembles with the underskin motions of the flesh becomes a stick without brains, refusing anything simple that is wanted of it. All that a rod has to do is lift the line, the leader, and the fly off the water, give them a good toss over the head, and then shoot them forward so they will land in the water without a splash in the following order: fly, transparent leader, and then the line—otherwise the fish will see the fly is a fake and be gone. Of course, there are special casts that anyone could predict would be difficult, and they require artistry—casts where the line can't go over the fisherman's head because cliffs or trees are immediately behind, sideways casts to get the fly under overhanging willows, and so on. But what's remarkable about just a straight cast—just picking up a rod with line on it and tossing the line across the river?

Well, until man is redeemed he will always take a fly rod too far back, just as natural man always overswings with an ax or golf club and loses all his power somewhere in the air; only with a rod it's worse, because the fly often comes so far back it gets caught behind in a bush or rock. When my father said it was an art that ended at two o'clock, he often added, "closer to twelve than to two," meaning that the rod should be taken back only slightly farther than overhead (straight overhead being twelve o'clock).

Then, since it is natural for man to try to attain power without recovering grace, he whips the line back and forth making it whistle each way, and sometimes even snapping off the fly from the leader, but the power that was going to transport the little fly across the river somehow gets diverted into building a bird's nest of line,

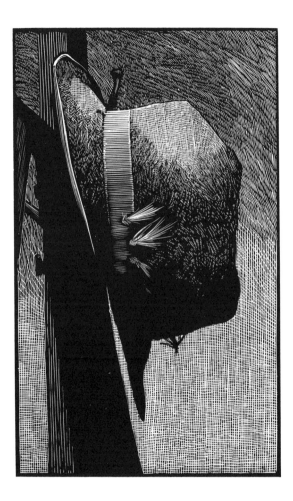

Paul's Fishing Hat

leader, and fly that falls out of the air into the water about ten feet in front of the fisherman. If, though, he pictures the round trip of the line, transparent leader, and fly from the time they leave the water until their return, they are easier to cast. They naturally come off the water heavy line first and in front, and light transparent leader and fly trailing behind. But, as they pass overhead, they have to have a little beat of time so the light, transparent leader and fly can catch up to the heavy line now starting forward and again fall behind it; otherwise, the line starting on its return trip will collide with the leader and fly still on their way up, and the mess will be the bird's nest that splashes into the water ten feet in front of the fisherman.

Almost the moment, however, that the forward order of line, leader, and fly is reestablished, it has to be reversed, because the fly and transparent leader must be ahead of the heavy line when they settle on the water. If what the fish sees is highly visible line, what the fisherman will see are departing black darts, and he might as well start for the next hole. High overhead, then, on the forward cast (at about ten o'clock) the fisherman checks again.

The four-count rhythm, of course, is functional. The one count takes the line, leader, and fly off the water; the two count tosses them seemingly straight into the sky; the three count was my father's way of saying that at the top the leader and fly have to be given a little beat of time to get behind the line as it is starting forward; the four count means put on the power and throw the line into the rod until you reach ten o'clock—then check-cast, let the fly and leader get ahead of the line, and coast to a soft and perfect landing. Power comes not from power everywhere, but from knowing where to put it on. "Remember," as my father kept saying, "it is an art that is performed on a four-count rhythm between ten and two o'clock."

My father was very sure about certain matters pertaining to the universe. To him, all good things—trout as well as eternal salvation—come by grace and grace comes by art and art does not come easy.

So my brother and I learned to cast Presbyterian-style, on a metronome. It was mother's metronome, which father had taken from the top of the piano in town. She would occasionally peer down to the dock from the front porch of the cabin, wondering nervously whether her metronome could float if it had to. When she became so overwrought that she thumped down the dock to reclaim it, my father would clap out the four-count rhythm with his cupped hands.

Eventually, he introduced us to literature on the subject. He tried always to say something stylish as he buttoned the glove on his casting hand. "Izaak Walton," he told us when my brother was thirteen or fourteen, "is not a respectable writer. He was an Episcopalian and a bait fisherman." Although Paul was three years younger than I was, he was already far ahead of me in anything relating to fishing and it was he who first found a copy of *The Compleat Angler* and reported back to me, "The bastard doesn't even know how to spell 'complete.' Besides, he has songs to sing to dairymaids." I borrowed his copy, and reported back to him, "Some of those songs are pretty good." He said, "Whoever saw a dairymaid on the Big Blackfoot River?

"I would like," he said, "to get him for a day's fishing on the Big Blackfoot—with a bet on the side."

The boy was very angry, and there has never been a doubt in my mind that the boy would have taken the Episcopalian money.

When you are in your teens—maybe throughout your life—being three years older than your brother often makes you feel he is a boy. However, I knew already that he was going to be a master with a rod. He had those extra things besides fine training—genius, luck, and plenty of self-confidence. Even at this age he liked to bet on himself against anybody who would fish with him, including me, his older brother. It was sometimes funny and sometimes not so funny, to see a boy always wanting to bet on himself and almost sure to win. Although I was three years older, I did not yet feel old enough to bet. Betting, I assumed, was for men who wore straw hats on the backs of their heads. So I was confused and embarrassed the first couple of times he asked me if I didn't want "a small bet on the side just to make things interesting." The third time he asked me must have made me angry because he never again spoke to me about money, not even about borrowing a few dollars when he was having real money problems.

We had to be very careful in dealing with each other. I often thought of him as a boy, but I never could treat him that way. He was never "my kid brother." He was a master of an art. He did not want any big brother advice or money or help, and, in the end, I could not help him.

Since one of the earliest things brothers try to find out is how they differ from each other, one of the things I remember longest about Paul is this business about his liking to bet. He would go to county fairs to pretend that he was betting on the horses, like the men, except that no betting booths would take his bets because they were too small and he was too young. When his bets were refused, he would say, as he said of Izaak Walton and any other he took as a rival, "I'd like to get that bastard on the Blackfoot for a day, with a bet on the side."

By the time he was in his early twenties he was in the big stud poker games.

Circumstances, too, helped to widen our differences. The draft of World War I immediately left the woods short of men, so at fifteen I started working for the United States Forest Service, and for many summers afterwards I worked in the woods, either with the Forest Service or in logging camps. I liked the woods and I liked work, but for a good many summers I didn't do much fishing. Paul was too young to swing an ax or pull a saw all day, and besides he had decided this early he had two major purposes in life: to fish and not to work, at least not allow work to interfere with fishing. In his teens, then, he got a summer job as a lifeguard at the municipal swimming pool, so in the early evenings he could go fishing and during the days he could look over girls in bathing suits and date them up for the late evenings.

When it came to choosing a profession, he became a

reporter. On a Montana paper. Early, then, he had come close to realizing life's purposes, which did not conflict in his mind from those given in answer to the first question in *The Westminster Catechism.*

Undoubtedly, our differences would not have seemed so great if we had not been such a close family. Painted on one side of our Sunday school wall were the words, God Is Love. We always assumed that these three words were spoken directly to the four of us in our family and had no reference to the world outside, which my brother and I soon discovered was full of bastards, the number increasing rapidly the farther one gets from Missoula, Montana.

We also held in common the knowledge that we were tough. This knowledge increased with age, at least until we were well into our twenties and probably longer, possibly much longer. But our differences showed even in our toughness. I was tough by being the product of tough establishments—the United States Forest Service and logging camps. Paul was tough by thinking he was tougher than any establishment. My mother and I watched horrified morning after morning while the Scottish minister tried to make his small child eat oatmeal. My father was also horrified—at first because a child of his own bowels would not eat God's oats, and, as the days went by, because his wee child proved tougher than he was. As the minister raged, the child bowed his head over the food and folded his hands as if his father were saying grace. The child gave only one sign of his own great anger. His lips became swollen. The hotter my father got, the colder the porridge, until finally my father burned out.

Each of us, then, not only thought he was tough, he knew the other one had the same opinion of himself. Paul knew that I had already been foreman of forest-fire crews and that, if he worked for me and drank on the job, as he did when he was reporting, I would tell him to go to camp, get his time slip, and keep on down the trail. I knew that there was about as much chance of his fighting fire as of his eating oatmeal.

We held in common one major theory about street fighting—if it looks like a fight is coming, get in the first punch. We both thought that most bastards aren't so tough as they talk—even bastards who look as well as talk tough. If suddenly they feel a few teeth loose, they will rub their mouths, look at the blood on their hands, and offer to buy a drink for the house. "But even if they still feel like fighting," as my brother said, "you are one big punch ahead when the fight starts."

There is just one trouble with this theory—it is only statistically true. Every once in a while you run into some guy who likes to fight as much as you do and is better at it. If you start off by loosening a few of his teeth he may try to kill you.

I suppose it was inevitable that my brother and I would get into one big fight which also would be the last one. When it came, given our theories about street fighting, it was like the Battle Hymn, terrible and swift. There are parts of it I did not see. I did not see our mother walk between us to try to stop us. She was short and wore glasses and, even with them on, did not have good vision. She had never seen a fight before or had any notion of how bad you can get hurt by becoming mixed up in one. Evidently, she just walked between her sons. The first I saw of her was the gray top of her head, the hair tied in a big knot with a big comb in it; but what was most noticeable was that her head was so close to Paul I couldn't get a good punch at him. Then I didn't see her anymore.

The fight seemed suddenly to stop itself. She was lying on the floor between us. Then we both began to cry and fight in a rage, each one shouting, "You son of a bitch, you knocked my mother down."

She got off the floor, and, blind without her glasses, staggered in circles between us, saying without recognizing which one she was addressing, "No, it wasn't you. I just slipped and fell."

So this was the only time we ever fought.

Perhaps we always wondered which of us was tougher, but, if boyhood questions aren't answered before a certain point in time, they can't ever be raised again. So we returned to being gracious to each other, as the wall suggested that we should be. We also felt that the woods and rivers were gracious to us when we walked together beside them.

It is true that we didn't often fish together anymore. We were both in our early thirties now, and "now" from here on is the summer of 1937. My father had retired and he and mother were living in Missoula, our old home town, and Paul was a reporter in Helena, the state capital. I had "gone off and got married," to use my brother's description of this event in my life. At the moment, I was living with my wife's family in the little town of Wolf

Creek, but, since Wolf Creek is only forty miles from Helena, we still saw each other from time to time, which meant, of course, fishing now and then together. In fact, the reason I had come to Helena now was to see him about fishing.

The fact also is that my mother-in-law had asked me to. I wasn't happy, but I was fairly sure my brother would finally say yes. He had never said plain no to me, and he loved my mother-in-law and my wife, whom he included in the sign on the wall, even though he could never understand "what had come over me" that would explain why marriage had ever crossed my mind.

I ran into him in front of the Montana Club, which was built by rich gold miners supposedly on the spot where gold was discovered in Last Chance Gulch. Although it was only ten o'clock in the morning, I had a hunch he was about to buy a drink. I had news to give him before I could ask the question.

After I gave him the news, my brother said, "He'll be just as welcome as a dose of clap."

I said to my brother, "Go easy on him. He's my brother-in-law."

My brother said, "I won't fish with him. He comes from the West Coast and he fishes with worms."

I said, "Cut it out. You know he was born and brought up in Montana. He just works on the West Coast. And now he's coming back for a vacation and writes his mother he wants to fish with us. With you especially."

My brother said, "Practically everybody on the West Coast was born in the Rocky Mountains where they failed as fly fishermen, so they migrated to the West Coast and became lawyers, certified public accountants, presidents of airplane companies, gamblers, or Mormon missionaries."

I wasn't sure he was about to buy a drink, but he had already had one.

We stood looking at each other, not liking anything that was happening but watching that we didn't go too far in disagreeing. Actually, though, we weren't very far apart about my brother-in-law. In some ways, I liked him even less than Paul did, and it's no pleasure to see your wife's face on somebody you don't like.

"Besides," my brother said, "he's a bait fisherman. All those Montana boys on the West Coast sit around the bars at night and lie to each other about their frontier childhood when they were hunters, trappers, and fly fishermen. But when they come back home they don't even kiss their mothers on the front porch before they're in the back garden with a red Hills Bros. coffee can digging for angleworms."

My brother and his editor wrote most of the Helena paper. The editor was one of the last small-town editors in the classic school of personal invective. He started drinking early in the morning so he wouldn't feel sorry for anyone during the day, and he and my brother admired each other greatly. The rest of the town feared them, especially because they wrote well, and in a hostile world both of them needed to be loved by their families and were.

I could tell by now that I was keeping my brother from

buying a drink, and, sure enough, he said, "Let's go in and hoist one."

I made the mistake of sounding as if I were afraid to come out and criticize his morals. I said, "I'm sorry, Paul, but it's too early in the morning for me to start drinking."

Having to say something else quick, I didn't improve my morals, at least not in my own eyes, by adding, "Florence asked me to ask you."

I hated to pass the buck to my mother-in-law. One reason Paul and I loved her was that she looked like our father. Both of them were Scots by way of Canada, both of them had blue eyes and sandy hair which was red when they were younger, and both of them pronounced "about" the way Canadians do, who, if they were poets, would rhyme it with "snoot."

I couldn't feel too sorry, though, because it really was she who had put me up to asking, and she had begun confusing me by mixing a certain amount of truth with her flattery. "Although I know nothing about fishing," she said, "I know Paul is the best fisherman anywhere." This was a complicated statement. She knew how to clean fish when the men forgot to, and she knew how to cook them, and, most important, she knew always to peer into the fisherman's basket and exclaim "My, my!" so she knew all that any woman of her time knew about fishing, although it is also true that she knew absolutely nothing about fishing.

"I would like very much to think of Neal with him and you," she concluded, no doubt hoping that we would improve his morals even more than his casting. In our

Brown Quill

Works best on slow-moving rivers like the Bitterroot River near Missoula and sixty miles south.

town, Paul and I were known as "the preacher's kids," and most mothers refrained from pointing us out to their children, but to this Scottish woman we were "the pastor's sons," and besides as fly fishermen we would be waist deep in cold water all day, where immorality is faced with some real but, as it turned out, not insurmountable problems.

"Poor boy," she said, adding as many Scottish *r*'s as she could to "poor." More than most mothers, Scottish mothers have had to accustom themselves to migration and sin, and to them all sons are prodigal and welcome home. Scotsmen, however, are much more reserved about welcoming returning male relatives, and do so largely under the powerful influence of their women.

"Sure I will," Paul said, "if Florence wants me to." And I knew that, having been given his word, I would never get another kick from him.

"Let's have a drink," I said, and at 10:15 A.M. I paid for it.

Just before 10:15 I told him Neal was coming to Wolf Creek day after tomorrow and that the day following we were to go fishing on the Elkhorn. "It's to be a family picnic," I told him.

"That's fine," he said. The Elkhorn is a small stream running into the Missouri and Paul and I were big-fish fishermen, looking with contempt upon the husbands of wives who have to say, "We like the little ones—they make the best eating." But the Elkhorn has many special features, including some giant Brown Trout that work their way up from the Missouri.

Although the Elkhorn was our favorite small stream, Paul said, after paying for our second drink, "I don't have to be on the beat tomorrow until evening, so what about just you and me taking the day off and fishing the big river before we have to go on the picnic?"

Paul and I fished a good many big rivers, but when one of us referred to "the big river" the other knew it was the Big Blackfoot. It isn't the biggest river we fished, but it is the most powerful, and per pound, so are its fish. It runs straight and hard—on a map or from an airplane it is almost a straight line running due west from its headwaters at Rogers Pass on the Continental Divide to Bonner, Montana, where it empties into the South Fork of the Clark Fork of the Columbia. It runs hard all the way.

Near its headwaters on the Continental Divide there is a mine with a thermometer that stopped at 69.7 degrees below zero, the lowest temperature ever officially recorded in the United States (Alaska omitted). From its headwaters to its mouth it was manufactured by glaciers. The first sixty-five miles of it are smashed against the southern wall of its valley by glaciers that moved in from the north, scarifying the earth; its lower twenty-five miles were made overnight when the great glacial lake covering northwestern Montana and northern Idaho broke its ice dam and spread the remains of Montana and Idaho mountains over hundreds of miles of the plains of eastern Washington. It was the biggest flood in the world for which there is geological evidence; it was so vast a geological event that the mind of man could only conceive of it but could not prove it until photographs could be taken from earth satellites.

The straight line on the map also suggests its glacial origins; it has no meandering valley, and its few farms are mostly on its southern tributaries which were not ripped up by glaciers; instead of opening into a wide flood plain near its mouth, the valley, which was cut overnight by a disappearing lake when the great ice dam melted, gets narrower and narrower until the only way a river, an old logging railroad, and an automobile road can fit into it is for two of them to take to the mountainsides.

It is a tough place for a trout to live—the river roars and the water is too fast to let algae grow on the rocks for feed, so there is no fat on the fish, which must hold most trout records for high jumping.

Besides, it is the river we knew best. My brother and I had fished the Big Blackfoot since nearly the beginning of the century—my father before then. We regarded it as a family river, as a part of us, and I surrender it now only with great reluctance to dude ranches, the unselected inhabitants of Great Falls, and the Moorish invaders from California.

Early next morning Paul picked me up in Wolf Creek, and we drove across Rogers Pass where the thermometer is that stuck at three-tenths of a degree short of seventy below. As usual, especially if it were early in the morning, we sat silently respectful until we passed the big Divide, but started talking the moment we thought we were draining into another ocean. Paul nearly always had a story to tell in which he was the leading character but not the hero.

He told his Continental Divide stories in a seemingly light-hearted, slightly poetical mood such as reporters often use in writing "human-interest" stories, but, if the mood were removed, his stories would appear as something about him that would not meet the approval of his family and that I would probably find out about in time anyway. He also must have felt honor-bound to tell me he lived other lives, even if he presented them to me as puzzles in the form of funny stories. Often I did not know what I had been told about him as we crossed the divide between our two worlds.

"You know," he began, "it's been a couple of weeks since I fished the Blackfoot." At the beginning, his stories sounded like factual reporting. He had fished alone and the fishing had not been much good, so he had to fish until evening to get his limit. Since he was returning directly to Helena he was driving up Nevada Creek along an old dirt road that followed section lines and turned at right angles at section corners. It was moonlight, he was tired and feeling in need of a friend to keep him awake, when suddenly a jackrabbit jumped on to the road and started running with the headlights. "I didn't push him too hard," he said, "because I didn't want to lose a friend." He drove, he said, with his head outside the window so he could feel close to the rabbit. With his head in the moonlight, his account took on poetic touches. The vague world of moonlight was pierced by the intense white triangle from the headlights. In the center of the penetrating isosceles was the jackrabbit, which, except for the length of his jumps, had become a snowshoe rabbit. The phosphorescent jackrabbit was doing his best to keep in the center of the isosceles but was afraid he was losing ground and, when he looked back to check, his eyes shone with whites and blues gathered up from the universe. My brother said, "I don't know how to explain what happened next, but there was a right-angle turn in this section-line road, and the rabbit saw it, and I didn't."

Later, he happened to mention that it cost him $175.00 to have his car fixed, and in 1937 you could almost get a car rebuilt for $175.00. Of course, he never mentioned that, although he did not drink when he fished, he always started drinking when he finished.

I rode part of the way down the Blackfoot wondering whether I had been told a little human-interest story with hard luck turned into humor or whether I had been told he had taken too many drinks and smashed hell out of the front end of his car.

Since it was no great thing either way, I finally decided to forget it, and, as you see, I didn't. I did, though, start thinking about the canyon where we were going to fish.

The canyon above the old Clearwater bridge is where the Blackfoot roars loudest. The backbone of a mountain would not break, so the mountain compresses the already powerful river into sound and spray before letting it pass. Here, of course, the road leaves the river; there was no place in the canyon for an Indian trail; even in 1806 when Lewis left Clark to come up the Blackfoot, he skirted the canyon by a safe margin. It is no place for small fish or small fishermen. Even the roar adds power to the fish or at least intimidates the fisherman.

When we fished the canyon we fished on the same side of it for the simple reason that there is no place in the canyon to wade across. I could hear Paul start to pass me to get to the hole above, and, when I realized I didn't hear him anymore, I knew he had stopped to watch me. Although I have never pretended to be a great fisherman, it was always important to me that I was a fisherman and looked like one, especially when fishing with my brother. Even before the silence continued, I knew that I wasn't looking like much of anything.

Although I have a warm personal feeling for the canyon, it is not an ideal place for me to fish. It puts a premium upon being able to cast for distance, and yet most of the time there are cliffs or trees right behind the fisherman so he has to keep all his line in front of him. It's like a baseball pitcher being deprived of his windup, and it forces the fly fisherman into what is called a "roll cast," a hard cast that I have never mastered. The fisherman has to work enough line into his cast to get distance without throwing any line behind him, and then he has to develop enough power from a short arc to shoot it out across the water.

He starts accumulating the extra amount of line for the long cast by retrieving his last cast so slowly that an unusual amount of line stays in the water and what is out of it forms a slack semiloop. The loop is enlarged by raising the casting arm straight up and cocking the wrist until it points to 1:30. There, then, is a lot of line in front of the fisherman, but it takes about everything he has to get it high in the air and out over the water so that the fly and leader settle ahead of the line—the arm is a piston, the wrist is a revolver that uncocks, and even the body gets behind the punch. Important, too, is the fact that the extra amount of line remaining in the water until the last moment gives a semisolid bottom to the cast. It is a little 1like a rattlesnake striking, with a good piece of his tail on the ground as something to strike from. All this is easy for a rattlesnake, but has always been hard for me.

Paul knew how I felt about my fishing and was careful not to seem superior by offering advice, but he had watched so long that he couldn't leave now without saying something. Finally he said, "The fish are out farther." Probably fearing he had put a strain on family relations, he quickly added, "Just a little farther."

I reeled in my line slowly, not looking behind so as not to see him. Maybe he was sorry he had spoken, but, having said what he said, he had to say something more. "Instead of retrieving the line straight toward you, bring it in on a diagonal from the downstream side. The diagonal will give you a more resistant base to your loop so you can put more power into your forward cast and get a little more distance."

Then he acted as if he hadn't said anything and I acted as if I hadn't heard it, but as soon as he left, which was immediately, I started retrieving my line on a diagonal, and it helped. The moment I felt I was getting a little more distance I ran for a fresh hole to make a fresh start in life.

It was a beautiful stretch of water, either to a fisherman or a photographer, although each would have focused his equipment on a different point. It was a barely submerged waterfall. The reef of rock was about two feet under the water, so the whole river rose into one wave, shook itself into spray, then fell back on itself and turned blue. After it recovered from the shock, it came back to see how it had fallen.

No fish could live out there where the river exploded into the colors and curves that would attract photographers. The fish were in that slow backwash, right in the dirty foam, with the dirt being one of the chief attractions. Part of the speckles would be pollen from pine trees, but most of the dirt was edible insect life that had not survived the waterfall.

I studied the situation. Although maybe I had just added three feet to my roll cast, I still had to do a lot of thinking before casting to compensate for some of my other shortcomings. But I felt I had already made the right beginning—I had already figured out where the big fish would be and why.

Then an odd thing happened. I saw him. A black back rose and sank in the foam. In fact, I imagined I saw spines on his dorsal fin until I said to myself, "God, he couldn't be so big you could see his fins." I even added, "You wouldn't even have seen the fish in all that foam if you hadn't first thought he would be there." But I couldn't shake the conviction that I had seen the black back of a big fish, because, as someone often forced to think, I know that often I would not see a thing unless I thought of it first.

Seeing the fish that I first thought would be there led me to wondering which way he would be pointing in the river. "Remember, when you make the first cast," I thought, "that you saw him in the backwash where the water is circling upstream, so he will be looking down-stream, not upstream, as he would be if he were in the main current."

I was led by association to the question of what fly I would cast, and to the conclusion that it had better be a large fly, a number four or six, if I was going after the big hump in the foam.

From the fly, I went to the other end of the cast, and asked myself where the hell I was going to cast from. There were only gigantic rocks at this waterfall, so I picked one of the biggest, saw how I could crawl up it, and knew from that added height I would get added distance, but then I had to ask myself, "How the hell am I going to land the fish if I hook him while I'm standing up there?" So I had to pick a smaller rock, which would shorten my distance but would let me slide down it with a rod in my hand and a big fish on.

I was gradually approaching the question all river fish-ermen should ask before they make the first cast, "If I hook a big one, where the hell can I land him?"

One great thing about fly fishing is that after a while nothing exists of the world but thoughts about fly fish-ing. It is also interesting that thoughts about fishing are often carried on in dialogue form where Hope and Fear—or, many times, two Fears—try to outweigh each other.

One Fear looked down the shoreline and said to me (a third person distinct from the two fears), "There is nothing but rocks for thirty years, but don't get scared and try to land him before you get all the way down to the first sandbar."

The Second Fear said, "It's forty, not thirty, yards

to the first sandbar and the weather has been warm and the fish's mouth will be soft and he will work off the hook if you try to fight him forty yards downriver. It's not good but it will be best to try to land him on a rock that is closer."

The First Fear said, "There is a big rock in the river that you will have to take him past before you land him, but, if you hold the line tight enough on him to keep him this side of the rock, you will probably lose him."

The Second Fear said, "But if you let him get on the far side of the rock, the line will get caught under it, and you will be sure to lose him."

That's how you know when you have thought too much—when you become a dialogue between *You'll probably lose* and *You're sure to lose*. But I didn't entirely quit thinking, although I did switch subjects. It is not in the book, yet it is human enough to spend a moment before casting in trying to imagine what the fish is thinking, even if one of its eggs is as big as its brain and even if, when you swim underwater, it is hard to imagine that a fish has anything to think about. Still, I could never be talked into believing that all a fish knows is hunger and fear. I have tried to feel nothing but hunger and fear and don't see how a fish could ever grow to six inches if that were all he ever felt. In fact, I go so far sometimes as to imagine that a fish thinks pretty thoughts. Before I made the cast, I imagined the fish with the black back lying cool in the carbonated water full of bubbles from the water-falls. He was looking downriver and watching the foam with food in it backing upstream like a floating cafeteria

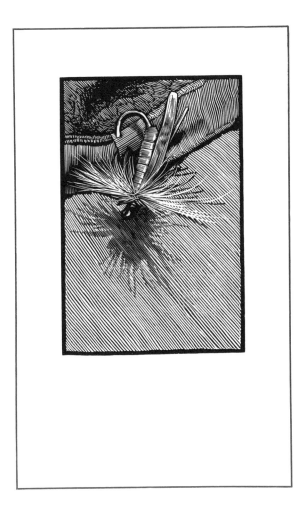

Salmon Quill

Matches the big hatch of the year—early June to early July. A specific fly used when floating version fails. Use this fly with underwater drift.

coming to wait on its customers. And he probably was imagining that the speckled foam was eggnog with nutmeg sprinkled on it, and, when the whites of eggs separated and he saw what was on shore, he probably said to himself, "What a lucky son of a bitch I am that this guy and not his brother is about to fish this hole."

I thought all these thoughts and some besides that proved of no value, and then I cast and I caught him.

I kept cool until I tried to take the hook out of his mouth. He was lying covered with sand on the little bar where I had landed him. His gills opened with his penultimate sighs. Then suddenly he stood up on his head in the sand and hit me with his tail and the sand flew. Slowly at first my hands began to shake, and, although I thought they made a miserable sight, I couldn't stop them. Finally, I managed to open the large blade to my knife which several times slid off his skull before it went through his brain.

Even when I bent him he was way too long for my basket, so his tail stuck out.

There were black spots on him that looked like crustaceans. He seemed oceanic, including barnacles. When I passed my brother at the next hole, I saw him study the tail and slowly remove his hat, and not out of respect to my prowess as a fisherman.

I had a fish, so I sat down to watch a fisherman.

He took his cigarettes and matches from his shirt pocket and put them in his hat and pulled his hat down tight so it wouldn't leak. Then he unstrapped his fish basket and hung it on the edge of his shoulder where he could get rid of it quick should the water get too big for him. If he studied the situation he didn't take any separate time to do it. He jumped off a rock into the swirl and swam for a chunk of cliff that had dropped into the river and parted it. He swam in his clothes with only his left arm—in his right hand, he held his rod high and sometimes all I could see was the basket and rod, and when the basket filled with water sometimes all I could see was the rod.

The current smashed him into the chunk of cliff and it must have hurt, but he had enough strength remaining in his left fingers to hang to a crevice or he would have been swept into the blue below. Then he still had to climb to the top of the rock with his left fingers and his right elbow which he used like a prospector's pick. When he finally stood on top, his clothes looked hydraulic, as if if they were running off him.

Once he quit wobbling, he shook himself duck-dog fashion, with his feet spread apart, his body lowered and his head flopping. Then he steadied himself and began to cast and the whole world turned to water.

Below him was the multitudinous river, and, where the rock had parted it around him, big-grained vapor rose. The mini-molecules of water left in the wake of his line made momentary loops of gossamer, disappearing so rapidly in the rising big-grained vapor that they had to be retained in memory to be visualized as loops. The spray emanating from him was finer-grained still and enclosed him in a halo of himself. The halo of himself was always there and always disappearing, as if he were candlelight flickering about three inches from himself. The images of himself and his line kept disappearing into the rising vapors of the river, which continually circled to the tops of the cliffs where, after becoming a wreath in the wind, they became rays of the sun.

The river above and below his rock was all big Rainbow water, and he would cast hard and low upstream, skimming the water with his fly but never letting it touch. Then he would pivot, reverse his line in a great oval above his head, and drive his line low and hard downstream, again skimming the water with his fly. He would complete this grand circle four or five times, creating an immensity of motion which culminated in nothing if you did not know, even if you could not see, that now somewhere out there a small fly was washing itself on a wave. Shockingly, immensity would return as the Big Blackfoot and the air above it became iridescent with the arched sides of a great Rainbow.

He called this "shadow casting," and frankly I don't know whether to believe the theory behind it—that the fish are alerted by the shadows of flies passing over the water by the first casts, so hit the fly the moment it touches the water. It is more or less the "working up an appetite" theory, almost too fancy to be true, but then every fine fisherman has a few fancy stunts that work for him and for almost no one else. Shadow casting never worked for me, but maybe I never had the strength of arm and wrist to keep line circling over the water until fish imagined a hatch of flies was out.

My brother's wet clothes made it easy to see his

strength. Most great casters I have known were big men over six feet, the added height certainly making it easier to get more line in the air in a bigger arc. My brother was only five feet ten, but he had fished so many years his body had become partly shaped by his casting. He was thirty-two now, at the height of his power, and he could put all his body and soul into a four-and-a-half-ounce magic totem pole. Long ago, he had gone far beyond my father's wrist casting, although his right wrist was always so important that it had become larger than his left. His right arm, which our father had kept tied to the side to emphasize the wrist, shot out of his shirt as if it were engineered, and it, too, was larger than his left arm. His wet shirt bulged and came unbuttoned with his pivoting shoulders and hips. It was also not hard to see why he was a street fighter, especially since he was committed to getting in the first punch with his right hand.

Rhythm was just as important as color and just as complicated. It was one rhythm superimposed upon another, our father's four-count rhythm of the line and wrist being still the base rhythm. But superimposed upon it was the piston two count of his arm and the long overriding four count of the completed figure eight of his reversed loop.

The canyon was glorified by rhythms and colors.

I heard voices behind me, and a man and his wife came down the trail, each carrying a rod, but probably they weren't going to do much fishing. Probably they intended nothing much more than to enjoy being out of doors with each other and, on the side, to pick enough huckleberries for a pie. In those days there was little in the way of rugged sports clothes for women, and she was a big, rugged woman and wore regular men's bib overalls, and her motherly breasts bulged out of the bib. She was the first to see my brother pivoting on the top of his cliff. To her, he must have looked something like a trick rope artist at a rodeo, doing everything except jumping in and out of his loops.

She kept watching while groping behind her to smooth out some pine needles to sit on. "My, my!" she said.

Her husband stopped and stood and said, "Jesus." Every now and then he said, "Jesus." Each time his wife nodded. She was one of America's mothers who never dream of using profanity themselves but enjoy their husbands', and later come to need it, like cigar smoke.

I started to make for the next hole. "Oh, no," she said, "you're going to wait, aren't you, until he comes to shore so you can see his big fish?"

"No," I answered, "I'd rather remember the molecules."

She obviously thought I was crazy, so I added, "I'll see his fish later." And to make any sense for her I had to add, "He's my brother."

As I kept going, the middle of my back told me that I was being viewed from the rear both as quite a guy, because I was his brother, and also as a little bit nutty, because I was molecular.

Since our fish were big enough to deserve a few drinks and quite a bit of talk afterwards, we were late in getting back to Helena. On the way, Paul asked, "Why not stay overnight with me and go down to Wolf Creek in the morning?" He added that he himself had "to be out for the evening," but would be back soon after midnight. I learned later it must have been around two o'clock in the morning when I heard the thing that was ringing, and I ascended through river mists and molecules until I awoke catching the telephone. The telephone had a voice in it, which asked, "Are you Paul's brother?" I asked, "What's wrong?" The voice said, "I want you to see him." Thinking we had poor connections, I banged the phone. "Who are you?" I asked. He said, "I am the desk sergeant who wants you to see your brother."

The checkbook was still in my hand when I reached the jail. The desk sergeant frowned and said, "No, you don't have to post bond for him. He covers the police beat and has friends here. All you have to do is look at him and take him home."

Then he added, "But he'll have to come back. A guy is going to sue him. Maybe two guys are."

Not wanting to see him without a notion of what I might see, I kept repeating, "What's wrong?" When the desk sergeant thought it was time, he told me, "He hit a guy and the guy is missing a couple of teeth and is all cut up." I asked, "What's the second guy suing him for?" "For breaking dishes. Also a table," the sergeant said. "The second guy owns the restaurant. The guy who got hit lit on one of the tables."

By now I was ready to see my brother, but it was becoming clear that the sergeant had called me to the station to have a talk. He said, "We're picking him up too much lately. He's drinking too much." I had already heard more than I wanted. Maybe one of our ultimate troubles was that I never wanted to hear too much about my brother.

The sergeant finished what he had to say by finally telling me what he really wanted to say, "Besides he's behind in the big stud poker game at Hot Springs. It's not healthy to be behind in the big game at Hot Springs.

"You and your brother think you're tough because you're street fighters. At Hot Springs they don't play any child games like fist fighting. At Hot Springs it's the big stud poker game and all that goes with it."

I was confused from trying to rise suddenly from molecules of sleep to an understanding of what I did not want to understand. I said, "Let's begin again. Why is he here and is he hurt?"

The sergeant said, "He's not hurt, just sick. He drinks too much. At Hot Springs, they don't drink too much." I said to the sergeant, "Let's go on. Why is he here?"

According to the sergeant's report to me, Paul and his girl had gone into Weiss's restaurant for a midnight sandwich—a popular place at midnight since it had booths in the rear where you and your girl could sit and draw the curtains. "The girl," the sergeant said, "was that half-breed Indian girl he goes with. You know the one," he added, as if to implicate me.

Paul and his girl were evidently looking for an empty booth when a guy in a booth they had passed stuck his head out of the curtain and yelled, "Wahoo." Paul hit the head, separating the head from two teeth and knocking the body back on the table, which overturned, cutting the guy and his girl with broken dishes. The sergeant said, "The guy said to me, 'Jesus, all I meant is that it's funny to go out with an Indian. It was just a joke.'"

38

I said to the sergeant, "It's not very funny," and the sergeant said, "No, not very funny, but it's going to cost your brother a lot of money and time to get out of it. What really isn't funny is that he's behind in the game at Hot Springs. Can't you help him straighten out?"

"I don't know what to do," I confessed to the sergeant.

"I know what you mean," the sergeant confessed to me. Desk sergeants at this time were still Irish. "I have a young brother," he said, "who is a wonderful kid, but he's always in trouble. He's what we call 'Black Irish.'"

"What do you do to help him?" I asked. After a long pause, he said, "I take him fishing."

"And when that doesn't work?" I asked.

"You better go and see your own brother," he answered.

Wanting to see him in perspective when I saw him, I stood still until I could again see the woman in bib overalls marveling at his shadow casting. Then I opened the door to the room where they toss the drunks until they can walk a crack in the floor. "His girl is with him," the sergeant said.

He was standing in front of a window, but he could not have been looking out of it, because there was a heavy screen between the bars, and he could not have seen me because his enlarged casting hand was over his face. Were it not for the lasting compassion I felt for his hand, I might have doubted afterwards that I had seen him.

His girl was sitting on the floor at his feet. When her black hair glistened, she was one of my favorite women. Her mother was a Northern Cheyene, so when her black hair glistened she was handsome, more Algonkian and Romanlike than Mongolian in profile, and very warlike, especially after a few drinks. At least one of her great grandmothers had been with the Northern Cheyennes when they and the Sioux destroyed General Custer and the Seventh Cavalry, and, since it was the Cheyennes who were camped on the Little Bighorn just opposite to the hill they were about to immortalize, the Cheyenne squaws were among the first to work the field over after the battle. At least one of her ancestors, then, had spent a late afternoon happily cutting off the testicles of the Seventh Cavalry, the cutting often occurring before death.

This paleface who had stuck his head out of the booth in Weiss's café and yelled "Wahoo" was lucky to be missing only two teeth.

Even I couldn't walk down the street beside her without her getting me into trouble. She liked to hold Paul with one arm and me with the other and walk down Last Chance Gulch on Saturday night, forcing people into the gutter to get around us, and when they wouldn't give up the sidewalk she would shove Paul or me into them. You didn't have to go very far down Last Chance Gulch on Saturday night shoving people into the gutter before you were into a hell of a big fight, but she always felt that she had a disappointing evening and had not been appreciated if the guy who took her out didn't get into a big fight over her.

When her hair glistened, though, she was worth it. She was one of the most beautiful dancers I have ever seen. She made her partner feel as if he were about to be left behind, or already had been.

It is a strange and wonderful and somewhat embarrassing feeling to hold someone in your arms who is trying to detach you from the earth and you aren't good enough to follow her.

I called her Mo-nah-se-tah, the name of the beautiful daughter of the Cheyenne chief, Little Rock. At first, she didn't particularly care for the name, which means, "the young grass that shoots in the spring," but after I explained to her that Mo-nah-se-tah was supposed to have had an illegitimate son by General George Armstrong Custer she took to the name like a duck to water.

Looking down on her now I could see only the spread of her hair on her shoulders and the spread of her legs on the floor. Her hair did not glisten and I had never seen her legs when they were just things lying on a floor. Knowing that I was looking down on her, she struggled to get to her feet, but her long legs buckled and her stockings slipped down on her legs and she spread out on the floor again until the tops of her stockings and her garters showed.

The two of them smelled worse than the jail. They smelled just like what they were—a couple of drunks whose stomachs had been injected with whatever it is the body makes when it feels cold and full of booze and knows something bad has happened and doesn't want tomorrow to come.

Neither one ever looked at me, and he never spoke. She

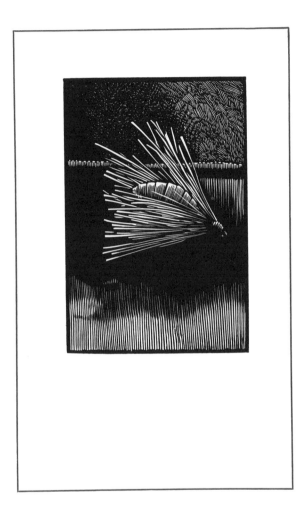

Yellow-Green Quill

Use small version as a Mayfly No. 8–10.

said, "Take me home." I said, "That's why I'm here."
She said, "Take him, too."

She was as beautiful a dancer as he was a fly caster. I
carried her with her toes dragging behind her. Paul
turned and, without seeing or speaking, followed. His
overdeveloped right wrist held his right hand over his
eyes so that in some drunken way he thought I could not
see him and he may also have thought that he could not
see himself.

As we went by the desk, the sergeant said, "Why don't
you all go fishing?"

I did not take Paul's girl to her home. In those days,
Indians who did not live on reservations had to live out by
the city limits and generally they pitched camp near
either the slaughterhouse or the city dump. I took them
back to Paul's apartment. I put him in his bed, and I put
her in the bed where I had been sleeping, but not until I
had changed it so that the fresh sheets would feel smooth
to her legs.

As I covered her, she said, "He should have killed the
bastard."

I said, "Maybe he did," whereupon she rolled over and
went to sleep, believing, as she always did, anything I
told her, especially if it involved heavy casualties.

By then, dawn was coming out of a mountain across the
Missouri, so I drove to Wolf Creek.

In those days it took about an hour to drive the forty
miles of rough road from Helena to Wolf Creek. While the
sun came out of the Big Belt Mountains and the Missouri
and left them behind in light, I tried to find something I

already knew about life that might help me reach out and touch my brother and get him to look at me and himself.

For a while, I even thought what the desk sergeant first told me was useful. As a desk sergeant, he had to know a lot about life and he had told me Paul was the Scottish equivalent of "Black Irish." Without doubt, in my father's family there were "Black Scots" occupying various outposts all the way from the original family home on the Isle of Mull in the southern Hebrides to Fairbanks, Alaska, 110 or 115 miles south of the Arctic Circle, which was about as far as a Scot could go then to get out of range of sheriffs with warrants and husbands with shotguns. I had learned about them from my aunts, not my uncles, who were all Masons and believed in secret societies for males. My aunts, though, talked gaily about them and told me they were all big men and funny and had been wonderful to them when they were little girls. From my uncles' letters, it was clear that they still thought of my aunts as little girls. Every Christmas until they died in distant lands these hastily departed brothers sent their once-little sisters loving Christmas cards scrawled with assurances that they would soon "return to the States and help them hang stockings on Christmas eve."

Seeing that I was relying on women to explain to myself what I didn't understand about men, I remembered a couple of girls I had dated who had uncles with some resemblances to my brother. The uncles were fairly expert at some art that was really a hobby—one uncle was a watercolorist and the other the club champion golfer—and each had selected a profession that would allow him to spend most of his time at his hobby. Both were charming, but you didn't quite know what if anything you knew when you had finished talking to them. Since they did not earn enough money from business to make life a hobby, their families had to meet from time to time with the county attorney to keep things quiet.

Sunrise is the time to feel that you will be able to find out how to help somebody close to you who you think needs help even if he doesn't think so. At sunrise everything is luminous but not clear.

Then about twelve miles before Wolf Creek the road drops into the Little Prickly Pear Canyon, where dawn is long in coming. In the suddenly returning semidarkness, I watched the road carefully, saying to myself, hell, my brother is not like anybody else. He's not my gal's uncle or a brother of my aunts. He is my brother and an artist and when a four-and-a-half-ounce rod is in his hand he is a major artist. He doesn't piddle around with a paint brush or take lessons to improve his short game and he won't take money even when he must need it and he won't run anywhere from anyone, least of all to the Arctic Circle. It is a shame I do not understand him.

Yet even in the loneliness of the canyon I knew there were others like me who had brothers they did not understand but wanted to help. We are probably those referred to as "our brothers' keepers," possessed of one of the oldest and possibly one of the most futile and certainly one of the most haunting of instincts. It will not let us go.

When I drove out of the canyon, it was ordinary daylight. I went to bed and had no trouble not going to sleep until my wife called me. "Don't forget," Jessie said, "you're going with Florence and me to meet Neal at the train." The truth was I had forgotten, but when I thought about him I felt relieved. It was good to remember that there was someone in my wife's family they worried about, and it was even better to remember that to me he was a little bit funny. I was in need of relief, and comic relief seemed about as good as any.

My wife kept standing at the door, waiting for me to roll over and try to go to sleep again. To her surprise, I jumped out of bed and started dressing. "It will be a pleasure," I told her. Jessie said to me, "You're funny," and I asked, "What's funny about me?" And Jessie said, "I know you don't like him." I said, "I do not like him," saying "do not" instead of "don't" in case my voice was blurred in waking up. Jessie said, "You're funny," and closed the door, then opened a crack of it and said, "You are not funny," and my wife's "not" was also distinct.

He was last off the train, and he came down the platform trying to remember what he thought an international-cup tennis player looked like. He undoubtedly was the first and last passenger ever to step off a Great Northern coach car at Wolf Creek, Montana, wearing white flannels and two sweaters. All this was in the days when the fancy Dans wore red-white-and-blue tennis sweaters, and he had a red-white-and-blue V-neck sweater over a red-white-and-blue turtleneck sweater. When he recognized us as relatives and realized that he couldn't be Bill Tilden or F. Scott Fitzgerald, he put down his suitcase and said, "Oh," except when he saw me he said nothing.

Then he turned his profile, and waited to be kissed. While the women took turns, I had a good look at his suitcase. It rested next to his elegant black-and-white shoes, and its straw sides had started to break open and one of its locks did not lock. Between its handles were the initials F. M., his mother's initials before she had married. When his mother saw the suitcase, she cried.

So he came home with about what he had when he left Montana, because he still had his mother's suitcase and his own conception of himself as a Davis Cup player, which had first come to the surface in Wolf Creek where you couldn't jump over a net without landing in cactus.

It was not until eight-thirty or nine that night that he tried to reduce himself in size so he could squeeze out of the door without being seen, but Florence and Jessie were waiting for him. My wife was barren of double-talk, so, to avoid being told, I got up and accompanied him to Black Jack's Bar, sometimes although rarely called a tavern.

Black Jack's was a freight car taken off its wheels and set on gravel at the other end of the bridge crossing the Little Prickly Pear. On the side of the box car was the sign of the Great Northern Railroad, a mountain goat gazing through a white beard on a world painted red. This is the only goat that ever saw the bottom of his world constantly occupied by a bottle of bar whiskey labeled "3-7-77," the number the Vigilantes pinned on the road agents they hanged in order to represent probably the dimensions of a grave. (The numbers are thought to mean three feet wide, seven feet long, and seventy-seven inches deep.) The bar was a log split in two by someone who wasn't much good with an ax, maybe Black Jack himself, but customers had done a much better job in greasing it with their elbows. Black Jack was short, trembled, and never got far from a revolver and a blackjack that lay behind the greased log. His teeth were bad, probably the result of drinking his own whiskey, which was made somewhere up Sheep Gulch.

The stools in front of the bar were reconstructed grocery crates. When Neal and I walked in, two of the crates were occupied, both by characters long familiar to the Great Northern goat. On the first was a bar character called Long Bow, because in this once Indian country anyone making an art of telling big lies about his hunting and shooting was said "to pull the long bow."

Having seen him shoot once, though, I myself never acted on the assumption that he lied about what he could do with firearms. I had seen a friend of his throw five aspirin tablets in the air which bloomed into five small white flowers immediately following five shots that sounded like one.

I was just as sure he could challenge the champion sheepherder of the Sieben ranch at his own game. The Sieben ranch is one of the finest in western Montana, spreading all the way from the Helena valley to Lincoln and beyond. Its owners, Jean and John Baucus, tell about a favorite sheepherder they once had to take to the hospital where his condition rapidly changed for the worse. They couldn't get his underwear off—it had been on him so long his hair had grown through it. Finally, they had to pluck him like a chicken, and when his underwear finally came off, pieces of skin came with it. At the opening of Long Bow's shirt, which wasn't buttoned for quite a way down, you could see hair sprouting out of his underwear.

On the crate at the other end of the bar was a female character known as Old Rawhide to the goats up and down the Great Northern line. About ten years before, at a Fourth of July celebration she had been elected beauty queen of Wolf Creek. She had ridden bareback standing up through the 111 inhabitants, mostly male, who had lined one of Wolf Creek's two streets. Her skirts flew high, and she won the contest. But, since she didn't quite have what it takes to become a professional rider, she did the next best thing. However, she still wore the divided skirts of a western horsewoman of the day, although they must have been a handicap in her new profession.

For a small town, Wolf Creek loomed large upon the map. It had two almost national celebrities, one a steer wrestler and the other a fancy roper. These two local artists spent their summers at county fairs and were good enough to come out five or six hundred dollars ahead for the season, less, of course, their hospital expenses. Old Rawhide did not intend to spend the rest of her life as a disappointed athlete, so she would shack up one winter with the fancy roper and the next winter with the steer wrestler. Occasionally, in late autumn when it looked as if it were going to be an especially hard winter, she would marry one of them, but marriage wasn't Old Rawhide's natural state of bliss, and before spring she would be shacked up with the other one. Shacking up brought out Old Rawhide's most enduring and durable qualities, and, unlike marriage, could be counted on to last all winter.

In the summers, while her artists were living off hot dogs at county fairs and rupturing their intestines while twisting the necks of steers, Old Rawhide inhabited Black Jack's Bar, reduced to picking up stray fishermen, most of them bait and hardware fishermen from Great Falls, so for her, as for the rest of the world, life had its ups and downs. However, she didn't show much the effects of life's gravitational pulls. Like many fancy riders, she was rather small and very tough and very strong, especially in the legs. She had weathered enough to deserve her name, but she didn't look much older than her thirty years spent mostly with horses and horsemen and the sporting element of Great Falls.

Even when she and Long Bow were at the bar, they sat at opposite ends so that itinerant fishermen had to sit between them and buy the drinks.

That's where Neal and I sat when we came in.

"Hi, Long Bow," Neal said, and overshook his hand. Long Bow did not like to be called Long Bow, although he knew he was called Long Bow behind his back, but to Neal he was just plain old Long Bow, and after a couple of shots of 3–7–77 Neal was outshooting, outhunting, and outtrapping the government trapper.

There was something deep in Neal that compelled him to lie to experts, even though they knew best that he was lying. He was one of those who need to be caught telling a lie while he is telling it.

As for Old Rawhide, Neal hadn't looked at her yet. I was already wise to the fact that Neal's opening ploy with women was to ignore them, and indeed was beginning to recognize what a good opening it is.

The mirror behind the bar looked like a polished Precambrian mudstone with ripples on it. Neal watched it constantly, evidently fascinated by the dark distorted image of himself living automatically—buying all the drinks and doing all the talking and none of the listening. I tried to break the monopoly by talking to Old Rawhide who was sitting next to me, but she was aware only of being ignored so she ignored me.

Finally, I listened, since no one would listen to me, although I didn't go so far as to buy the drinks. Neal had trailed an otter and her pups up to Rogers Pass, where the thermometer officially recorded 69.7 degrees below zero. While he trailed this otter, I tried to trace its lineage from his description of it. "I had a hard time following it," he said, "because it had turned white in the winter," so it must have been part ermine. After he treed her, he said, "She stretched out on the lower branch ready to pounce on the first deer that came along," so she had to have a strain of mountain lion in her. She also must have been part otter, because she was jokey and smiled at him. But mostly she was 3–7–77, because she was the only animal in western Montana besides man that had pups in the winter. "They snuggled up right in my shirt," he said, showing us a shirt under his two red-white-and-blue sweaters.

Long Bow gently tapped the thick bottom of his empty

glass on the bar, without saying a word for fear of appearing inattentive. But Old Rawhide couldn't stand the silent treatment any longer, no matter what. She leaned in front of me and said to the side of Neal's face, "Hey, Buster, what are otters doing on the top of the Continental Divide? I thought otters swam in creeks and played on mud slides?"

Neal stopped in the middle of a sentence and stared at the mirror, trying to pick out the distortion other than his own which had spoken. "Let's have another drink," he said to all the distortions. Then for the first time he formally recognized that a woman was present by looking not at the image but at the reality of Black Jack behind the bar, and saying, "Give her one, too."

Old Rawhide closed her hand when a drink was put in it, but kept on staring at Neal's profile. In the ranch town of Wolf Creek, she and the Great Northern goat had probably seen only a couple of other men who were pale and had sunken eyes.

As I pushed myself out of my crate to keep my promise to go home early, Long Bow said, "Thanks." Since I hadn't bought a drink all evening, I knew he must be thanking me for leaving them my brother-in-law. The moment I rose from my crate, Old Rawhide moved into it to be closer to Neal. She peered into his profile, and romance stirred under her epidermis.

On the way out, I said to Neal over my shoulder, "Don't forget, you're going fishing tomorrow morning," and he looked over her shoulder and said, "What?"

Paul Maclean

Paul was in Wolf Creek early next morning, just as he said he would be. Although he and I had acquired freedoms as we grew up, we never violated our early religious training of always being on time for church, work, and fishing.

Florence met him at the door and said nervously, "I'm sorry, Paul, but Neal isn't up yet. He got home late."

Paul said, "I didn't even go to bed last night. Get him up, Florence."

She said, "He isn't very well."

He said, "Neither am I, but I am going fishing in a few minutes."

They stared at each other. No Scottish mother likes to be caught with a lazy son in bed, and no Scot going fishing likes to stand around waiting for a male relative with a hangover. Although the Scots invented whiskey, they try not to acknowledge the existence of hangovers, especially within the family circle. Normally, it would have been no better than a standoff between my brother and my mother-in-law, but in this rare case a Scottish lady couldn't think of a thing to say in her son's defense, so she had to wake him up, although as little as possible.

We slowly loaded the half-ton truck that belonged to Kenny, my one brother-in-law who had remained in Wolf Creek. The three women had already covered the shady end of the box with an old mattress, and then they covered the mattress with their relative from the West Coast. After space had been found for the potato salad, the grill and our fishing tackle, six of us tried to be comfortable without in any way disturbing the mattress.

All but the first three miles of the road to the Elkhorn parallels the Missouri as it emerges from the gigantic opening that Lewis and Clark called the Gateway to the Mountains. Although the water remains clear for a few miles farther down, the earth itself turns tawny almost the moment the river pours out of the mountains. It is just below the dark opening where the Elkhorn empties into the Missouri that the road ends. Like most dirt roads paralleling the Missouri, it is mostly gray dust and chuckholes. The chuckholes did not improve Neal's health, and the gray dust would turn to gumbo if it rained.

Kenny, as the one of Jessie's brothers who stayed in Wolf Creek, was like most who live in towns with two streets—he could do nearly anything with his hands. Among other things, he could drive a half-ton truck over country where it would be hard to take a pack mule, and he had married Dorothy, a registered nurse. She was short and powerful and had been trained as a surgical nurse. Ranchers holding their intestines in their hands would ride in from the back country looking for "the RN" to sew them together again. Florence and Jessie were also medical in varying degrees, and the three of them were thought of as the medical center of Wolf Creek. Now, the three women bent over an old mattress, constituting, as it were, the intensive-care unit.

Ken was friendly with all 111 inhabitants of Wolf Creek and most of the ranchers in the surrounding country, especially with the ranchers from Scotland, who had come to the West early, knowing ahead of time how to raise cattle in mountains and snow. That's how we got permission to fish in the Elkhorn. Jim McGregor owned it to its headwaters, and every fence was posted, reading from top to bottom, "No Hunting," "No Fishing," and finally, as an afterthought, "No Trespassing." As a result, he furnished pasture for about as many elk as cows, but he figured this was cheaper than opening his range to hunters from Great Falls who have difficulty telling an elk from a cow.

One thing about a ranch road—there is less and less of it the closer it gets to the cows. It became just two ruts that made switchbacks to the top of a ridge, and then it repeated roughly the same number down to the Elkhorn, which is just a curve of willows and water winding through high grass until suddenly a mountain opens and the willows disappear. At the top of the ridge the ruts were still made of gray dust, and black clouds rested upon the black mountains ahead.

Paul was out of the truck as soon as it stopped at the creek bottom. He had his rod up and his leader and flies on before I could free myself from the vise in which I had been sitting between Dorothy and Jessie, who had been holding me tight by the soft part of the arm and muttering, "Don't you run off and leave my brother." Besides, I had to hop around for a minute or so, because a leg had gone to sleep in the vise.

By that time, Paul was saying behind his back, "I'll walk three fishing distances down and then fish upstream. You spread out and fish downstream until we meet." Then he was gone.

One reason Paul caught more fish than anyone else was

that he had his flies in the water more than anyone else. "Brother," he would say, "there are no flying fish in Montana. Out here, you can't catch fish with your flies in the air." His outfit was set up ready to go the moment he stepped out of the car; he walked fast; he seldom wasted time changing flies but instead changed the depth he was fishing them or the motion with which he retrieved them; if he did change flies, he tied knots with the speed of a seamstress; and so on. His flies were in the water at least twenty percent more of the time than mine.

I guessed there was also another reason why today he was separating himself from me as fast and as far as possible—he did not want me to talk to him about the other night.

Ken said he would go upstream to fish the beaver dams. He liked beaver dams and he knew how to fish them. So off he went happily to wade in ooze and to get throttled by brush and to fall through loose piles of sticks called beaver dams and to end up with a wreath of seaweed round his neck and a basketful of fish.

Jessie gave me another pinch on the arm and shortened her warning to, "Don't leave my brother." Rubbing my arm, I made him go first so he couldn't escape immediately. We went down the trail around the first bend where the creek comes out of osiers and crosses a meadow. Then his steps faltered and became intentionally pitiful. "I'm still not well," he said; "I think I'll stop here and fish the meadow." Because of the bend in the creek, he couldn't be seen, and yet, if he walked back, he would have only a couple of hundred yards to go.

"Why not?" I asked, already knowing a foolish question when I asked one.

Even though Paul must have had three or four fish by now, I took my time walking down the trail, trying with each step to leave the world behind. Something within fishermen tries to make fishing into a world perfect and apart—I don't know what it is or where, because sometimes it is in my arms and sometimes in my throat and sometimes nowhere in particular except somewhere deep. Many of us probably would be better fishermen if we did not spend so much time watching and waiting for the world to become perfect.

The hardest thing usually to leave behind, as was the case now, can loosely be called the conscience.

Should or shouldn't I speak to my brother about what happened the other night? I referred to it vaguely as "what happened the other night" so as not to visualize it, especially not the casting hand. Shouldn't I at least offer to help him with money, if he has to pay damages? I thought about these old questions in new forms now framed by long dancing legs spread on a jail floor until finally the questions of conscience disappeared, again as usual, without any answers to them. I still didn't know whether I had resolved to talk to my brother today.

However, I still kept worrying about something, whatever it was, until I turned around in the trail and went back to the meadow so I could say that I had.

Across the meadow was a dam and above it a big blue hole where Neal sat nodding on a rock, the red Hills Bros. coffee can beside him. His neck was bowed, pale, exposed to the sun and soon to match the coffee can.

"What are you doing?" I asked.

It took him some time to arrange an answer. "I have been fishing," he said finally. Then he tried over again for greater accuracy. "I have been fishing and not feeling well," he said.

"This dead water isn't much of a place to fish, is it?" I asked.

"Why," he said, "look at all those fish at the bottom of the hole."

"Those are squaw fish and suckers," I told him, without looking.

"What's a sucker?" he asked, and so became the first native of Montana ever to sit on a rock and ask what a sucker was.

In the deep water below him was a little botch of pink that was sure to be angleworms with one hook running through all their guts. On the leader, just above the worms, were two red beads, strung there no doubt for cosmetic purposes. The botch of angleworms and the two beads hung within six inches of the nearest sucker. Not a fish stirred, and neither did the fisherman, although both were in plain view of each other.

"Would you like to go fly fishing sometime with Paul and me?" I asked.

"Thanks," he said, "but not just now."

"Well, then," I said, "take care of yourself and have a good time."

"I am," he said.

I walked down the trail again under the mistaken notion I might have done myself some good by going back to see my brother-in-law. However, that big cloud coming out of the entrance to the Rocky Mountains kept telling me that, much as I was looking for moments of perfection, I wasn't going to find any today. And also that I wasn't going to catch many fish unless I quit fooling around.

I turned off the trail at the next meadow, and could have caught my limit in two or three holes. Because Jim McGregor allowed only a few fishermen a year on this small creek, it was overpopulated with fish that would probably never grow longer than ten or eleven inches.

I had only one problem in catching them and it lasted for only the first few fish. I was too fast in setting the hook. There is a barb on the end of the hook, and unless the hook gets imbedded in the fish's mouth or jaw deep enough to "set" the barb in it, the fish spits or tears the hook out. So, as the fish strikes, the line has to be given a little jerk, either directly with the left hand or with the rod in the right hand. The timing and the pressure have to be perfect—too soon or too late or too little or too much and the fish may have a sore mouth for a few days but will probably live longer for his experience.

I was setting the fly so fast I was taking it away from the fish before they could get hold of it. Every different kind of trout is on a different speedometer, and the correct timing will vary also with the stream and even the weather and time of day. I had been fishing too long in the fast water of the Big Blackfoot where big Rainbows charge out from behind the fortresses of big rocks. Some early rancher had planted the Elkhorn with Eastern Brook

Trout, and, as the name suggests, they are a more meditative type.

Once I got my timing slowed down, I lost interest in them. They are beautiful to see—black backs, yellow and orange spots on their sides, red bellies ending in under-fins fringed with white. They are compositions in colors, and were often painted on platters. But they are only fairly good fighters and they feel like eels because their scales are so small. Besides, their name is against them in western Montana where the word "brook" is not a socially acceptable substitute for "creek."

All of a sudden I wondered what my brother was doing because I knew he certainly wasn't wasting time catching his limit of ten-inch Eastern Brook Trout. If I wanted to stay in shooting distance of him, I had better start trying to catch some of those Brown monsters that work their way up from the Missouri.

Fishing is a world created apart from all others, and inside it are special worlds of their own—one is fishing for big fish in small water where there is not enough world and water to accommodate a fish and a fisherman, and the willows on the side of the creek are all against the fisherman.

I stopped, cleaned my Eastern Brook Trout, and arranged them in my basket between layers of wild hay and mint where they were more beautiful than those painted on platters. Then, in preparation for big game, I changed to an eight-pound test leader and to a number six fly.

I waxed the first thirty feet of my line in case it had

become water-soaked and would not float, took one final look at my ten-inch Eastern Brook Trout lying in mint, and then closed my basket on the world of small fish.

A huge shadow met me coming across the meadow, with one big cloud behind it. The Elkhorn Canyon is so deep and narrow that a black cloud or a cloud and a half can constitute the sky. The black cloud and a half can pass on to sunshine or it can make room for blacker clouds. From the bottom of the canyon, there is no way of seeing what is coming, but I had a feeling it wasn't sunshine.

Suddenly, so many fish began to jump that it looked as if the first extra-large raindrops had arrived. When fish start jumping like this, something is happening to the weather.

At that moment, the world was totally composed of the Elkhorn, a mythological Brown Trout, the weather and me, and all that existed of me were thoughts about the Elkhorn, the weather, and a mythological fish that may have been a fingerling of my imagination.

The Elkhorn looks just like what it is—a crack in the earth to mark where the Rocky Mountains end and the Great Plains begin. The giant mountains are black-backed with nearly the last of mountain pines. Their eastern sides turn brown and yellow as the tall prairie grasses begin, but there are occasional black spots where the pines scatter themselves out to get a last look back. The mythological Brown Trout and the canyon harmonized in my thoughts. The trout that might be real and close at hand was massive, black on the back, yellow and brown on the sides, had black spots and a final fringe of white. The Elkhorn and the Brown Trout are also alike in being beautiful by being partly ugly.

I walked past 150 or 200 yards of water where little "Brookies" were still bouncing like rain and came finally to a beautiful stretch with not a fish jumping in it. At the head of the hole the water parted on a big rock, swirled backwards, deepened, deposited, and finally lost depth and motion by drifting under osiers. I thought, it can't be that no fish jumps in such beautiful water because no fish is in it. It must be one fish is there so big he is like a bull elk with "a royal head" that in rutting season runs all male contenders out of the herd.

Since it is generally better to fish creeks upstream so the water to be fished next is not dirtied, I stepped back on shore where the fish couldn't see me and walked to the lower end of the hole before making my first cast. By then, I had lost faith in my theory about the one bull elk in the hole, but I did expect to pick up a Brookie or two in the shallow water. When I didn't create a stir, I moved upstream to deeper water where the osiers began and bugs dropped off them.

Not even a glitter in the water from the side of a trout that started for the fly and suddenly decided that something looked wrong. I began to wonder if somebody had thrown a stick of dynamite into the hole and had blown all the fish belly up, along with my one bull-elk theory. If there was one fish in all this water, there was only one place left for him to be—if he wasn't in the open water and if he wasn't around the edges of the osiers, then he had to be under the osiers, and I wasn't happy about the prospect of casting into willow bushes.

Grey Quill

Best all-around fly. Size 10–6.
Lake or stream.

Years ago at the end of a summer that I had worked in the Forest Service I was fishing with Paul, and, being out of practice, I was especially careful to keep in open water. Paul watched me fish a hole that went under willows until he couldn't bear the sight any longer.

"Brother," he said, "you can't catch trout in a bathtub.

"You like to fish in sunny, open water because you are a Scot and afraid to lose a fly if you cast into the bushes.

"But the fish are not taking sunbaths. They are under the bushes where it is cool and safe from fishermen like you."

I only supported his charges in defending myself. "I lose flies when I get mixed up in the bushes," I complained.

"What the hell do you care?" he asked. "We don't pay for flies. George is always glad to tie more for us. Nobody," he said, "has put in a good day's fishing unless he leaves a couple of flies hanging on the bushes. You can't catch fish if you don't dare go where they are.

"Let me have your rod," he said. I suppose he took my rod so I wouldn't think that the cast into the bushes could be done only by his rod. It was in this way that I came to know that my rod can be made to cast into bushes, but the truth is I have never mastered the cast, probably because I still flinch from the prospect of losing flies that I don't have to pay for.

I had no choice now but to cast into the willows if I wanted to know why fish were jumping in the water all around me except in this hole, and I still wanted to know, because it is not fly fishing if you are not looking for answers to questions.

Since I hadn't used this cast for some time, I decided to practice up a bit, so I dropped downstream to make a few casts into the bushes. Then I walked cautiously upstream to where the osiers were thickest, watching my feet and not rattling any rocks.

The cast was high and soft when it went by my head, the opposite of what it would have been if it was being driven into the wind. I was excited, but kept my arm cool and under my control. Instead of putting on power as the line started forward, I let it float on until the vertical periscope in my eye or brain or arm or wherever it is told me my fly was over the edge of the nearest osiers. Then I put a check cast into the line, and it began to drop almost straight down. Ten or fifteen feet before the fly lights, you can tell whether a cast like this is going to be perfect, and, if necessary, still make slight corrections. The cast is so soft and slow that it can be followed like an ash settling from a fireplace chimney. One of life's quiet excitements is to stand somewhat apart from yourself and watch yourself softly becoming the author of something beautiful, even if it is only a floating ash.

The leader settled on the lowest branch of the bush and the fly swung on its little pendulum three or four inches from the water, or maybe it was five or six. To complete the cast, I was supposed next to shake the line with my rod, so, if the line wasn't caught in the bush, the fly would drop into the water underneath. I may have done this, or maybe the fish blew out of the water and took my fly as it soared up the bush. It is the only time I have ever fought a fish in a tree.

Indians used to make baskets out of the red branches of

osiers, so there was no chance the branches would break. It was fish or fisherman.

Something odd, detached, and even slightly humorous happens to a big-fish fisherman a moment after a big fish strikes. In the arm, shoulder, or brain of a big-fish fisherman is a scale, and the moment the big fish goes in the air the big-fish fisherman, no matter what his blood pressure is, places the scale under the fish and coolly weighs him. He doesn't have hands and arms enough to do all the other things he should be doing at the same time, but he tries to be fairly exact about the weight of the fish so he won't be disappointed when he catches him. I said to myself, "This son of a bitch weighs seven or eight pounds," and I tried to allow for the fact that I might be weighing part of the bush.

The air was filled with dead leaves and green berries from the osiers, but their branches held. As the big Brown went up the bush, he tied a different knot on every branch he passed. He wove that bush into a basket with square knots, bowlines, and double half hitches.

The body and spirit suffer no more sudden visitation than that of losing a big fish, since, after all, there must be some slight transition between life and death. But, with a big fish, one moment the world is nuclear and the next it has disappeared. That's all. It has gone. The fish has gone and you are extinct, except for four and a half ounces of stick to which is tied some line and a semitransparent thread of catgut to which is tied a little curved piece of Swedish steel to which is tied a part of a feather from a chicken's neck.

I don't even know which way he went. As far as I know,

he may have gone right on up the bush and disappeared into thin air.

I waded out to the bush to see if any signs of reality had been left behind. There was some fishing tackle strung around, but my hands trembled so I couldn't untie the complicated knots that wove it into the branches.

Even Moses could not have trembled more when his bush blew up on him. Finally, I untied my line from the leader and left the rest of the mess in the willows.

Poets talk about "spots of time," but it is really fishermen who experience eternity compressed into a moment. No one can tell what a spot of time is until suddenly the whole world is a fish and the fish is gone. I shall remember that son of a bitch forever.

A voice said, "He was a big one." It could have been my brother, or it could have been the fish circling back in the air and bragging about himself behind my back.

I turned and said to my brother, "I missed him." He had seen it all, so if I had known of something else I would have mentioned it. Instead, I repeated, "I missed him." I looked down at my hands, and the palms were turned up, as if in supplication.

"There wasn't anything you could have done about it," he said. "You can't catch a big fish in the brush. In fact, I never saw anyone try it before."

I figured he was just trying to sprinkle me with comfort, especially when I couldn't help seeing a couple of gigantic brown tails with gigantic black spots sticking out of his basket. "How did you catch yours?" I asked. I was very excited, and asked whatever I wanted to know.

He said, "I got them in shallow, open water where there weren't any bushes."

I asked, "Big ones like that in shallow, open water?"

He said, "Yes, big Brown Trout. You are used to fishing for big Rainbow in big water. But big Browns often feed along the edges of a bank in a meadow where grasshoppers and even mice fall in. You walk along the shallow water until you can see black backs sticking out of it and mud swirling."

This left me even more dismayed. I thought that I had fished the hole perfectly and just the way my brother had taught me, except he hadn't told me what to do when a fish goes up a tree. That's one trouble with hanging around a master—you pick up some of his stuff, like how to cast into a bush, but you use it just when the master is doing the opposite.

I was still excited. There was still some great hollow inside me to be filled and needed the answer to another question. Until I asked it, I had no idea what it would be. "Can I help you with money or anything?" I asked.

Alarmed by hearing myself, I tried to calm down quickly. Instead, having made a mistake, I made it worse. "I thought you might need some help because of the other night," I said.

Probably he took my reference to the other night as a reference to his Indian girl, so, to change the subject, I said, "I thought maybe it cost you a lot to fix the front end of your car the night you chased the rabbit." Now I had made three mistakes.

He acted as if his father had offered to help him to a

bowl of oatmeal. He bowed his head in silence until he was sure I wouldn't say anything more. Then he said, "It's going to rain."

I glanced at the sky which I had forgotten about since the world had become no higher than a bush. There was a sky above all right, but it was all one black cloud that must have been a great weight for the canyon to bear.

My brother asked, "Where's Neal?"

The question caught me by surprise, and I had to think until I found him. "I left him at the first bend," I said finally.

"You'll get hell for that," my brother told me.

That remark enlarged my world until it included a half-ton truck and several Scottish women. "I know," I replied, and started taking my rod down. "I'm through for the day," I said, nodding at my rod.

Paul asked, "Do you have your limit?" I said, "No," even though I knew he was asking if I wasn't already in enough trouble without quitting short of my limit. To women who do not fish, men who come home without their limit are failures in life.

My brother also felt much the same way. "It would take you only a few minutes to finish up your limit with Brookies," he said, "they are still jumping all over. I'll smoke a cigarette while you catch six more."

I said, "Thanks, but I'm through for the day," although I knew he couldn't understand why six more little Eastern Brook Trout would make no difference in my view of life. Clearly by now it was one of those days when the world outside wasn't going to let me do what I really wanted to do—catch a big Brown Trout and talk to my brother in some helpful way. Instead there was an empty bush and it was about to rain.

Paul said, "Come on, let's go and find Neal." Then he added, "You shouldn't have left him behind."

"What?" I asked.

"You should try to help him," he replied.

I could find words but not sentences they could fit. "I didn't leave him. He doesn't like me. He doesn't like Montana. He left me to go bait fishing. He can't even bait-fish. Me, I don't like anything about him."

I could feel all the excitement of losing the big fish going through the transformer and coming out as anger at my brother-in-law. I could also feel that I was repeating myself without quite saying the same thing. Even so, I asked, "Do you think you should help him?"

"Yes," he said, "I thought we were going to."

"How?" I asked.

"By taking him fishing with us."

"I've just told you," I said, "he doesn't like to fish."

"Maybe so," my brother replied. "But maybe what he likes is somebody trying to help him."

I still do not understand my brother. He himself always turned aside any offer of help, but in some complicated way he was surely talking about himself when he was talking about Neal needing help. "Come on," he said, "let's find him before he gets lost in the storm." He tried to put his arm around my shoulders but his fish basket with big tails sticking out of it came between us and made it difficult. We both looked clumsy—I in trying to offer him help, and he in trying to thank me for it.

"Let's get a move on," I said. We hit the trail and

started upstream. The black cloud was taking over the canyon completely. The dimensions of the world were compressed to about 900′ x 900′ x 900′. It must have been something like this in 1949 when the giant fire from Mann Gulch, the next gulch up the Missouri, swept over the divide into the Elkhorn. Mann Gulch was where the Forest Service dropped sixteen of its crack smoke jumpers, thirteen of whom had to be identified later by their dental work. That's the way the storm came down the Elkhorn—about to obliterate it.

As if a signal had been given, not a fish jumped. Then the wind came. The water left the creek and went up in the bushes, like my fish. The air along the creek was filled with osier leaves and green berries. Then the air disappeared from view. It was present only as cones and branches that struck my face and kept going.

The storm came on a wild horse and rode over us.

We started across the meadow at the bend to look for Neal but soon we weren't even sure where we were. My lips ran with wet water. "The bastard isn't here," I said, although neither of us knew exactly where "here" was. "No," my brother said, "he's there." Then he added, "And dry." So we both knew where "there" was.

By the time we got back to the truck the rain had become steady, controlled now by gravity. Paul and I had put our cigarettes and matches inside our hats to keep them dry, but I could feel the water running around the roots of my hair.

The truck emerged out of the storm as if out of the pioneer past, looking like a covered wagon besieged by circling rain. Ken must have hurried back from the beaver

dams in time to get out a couple of old tarpaulins, cut
some poles and then stretch the tarps over the box of the
truck. It was up to me and not my brother to be the first
to poke my head through the canvas and be the "African
dodger" in the sideshow at the old circus who stuck his
head through a canvas drop and let anyone throw a baseball at it for a dime. With my head in the hole, however,
I froze, powerless to duck anything that might be thrown
or even to determine the order in which things appeared.
The actual order turned out not to be of my choosing.

First it was the women who appeared and then the old
mattress, the women appearing first because two of them
held carving knives and the other, my wife, held a long
fork, all of which glittered in the semidarkness under the
tarps. The women squatted on the floor of the box, and
had been making sandwiches until they saw my head
appear like a target on canvas. Then they pointed their
cutlery at me.

In the middle of the box there was a leak where the
tarps sagged and did not quite come together. Behind in
the far end of the box was the old mattress, but, because
of the cutlery, I couldn't see it in detail.

My wife said, pointing the long fork at me, "You went
off and left him."

My mother-in-law, stroking her knife on steel, said,
"Poor boy, he's not well. He was exposed to the sun
too long."

With the only words I was able to utter while my
throat was in this exposed position, I asked, "Is that what
he told you?"

"Yes, poor boy," she said, and wiggled to the rear of

the box and stroked his head with one hand while keeping a firm hold on the carving knife with the other. Being short a hand, she left the steel behind.

The cracks between the tarps let in a lot of water but not much light, so it took some time for my eyes to get adjusted to my brother-in-law lying on the mattress. The light first picked up his brow, which was serene but pale, as mine would have been if my mother had spent her life in making me sandwiches and protecting me from reality.

My brother stuck his head through the tarps and stood beside me. It made me feel better having a representative of my family present. I thought, "Some day I hope I can help him as much."

The women made my brother a sandwich. As for me, my head and shoulders were under cover, but the rest of me might as well have been under a rain spout. Paul was in the same shape, and no one made a move to push closer together and make room for us inside. The bastard had the whole upper end of the box to himself. Instead of lying all over the mattress, all he had to do was sit up.

Outside, the water came down my back on a wide front, crowded into a narrow channel across my rear end, and then divided into two branches and emptied into my socks.

When the women weren't using their hardware to make sandwiches for Neal they were pointing it at me. I could smell all the sandwiches they weren't making for me and I could smell water leaking through canvas and turning to vapor from the warmth of crowded bodies and

Santa Claus Streamer

Yields a few gifts when nothing else works.
White polar bear hair gives fly good motion
plus radiancy.

I could also smell the vapor of last night's booze rising from the old mattress. You probably know that Indians build their sweat baths on the banks of rivers. After they become drenched with sweat they immediately jump into the cold water outside, and, it may be added, sometimes they immediately die. I felt that at the same time I was both halves of myself and a sweat bath and a cold river and about to die.

I entertained a series of final thoughts. "How could the bastard suffer from too much sun? The bastard hasn't seen more than a couple of hours of sunlight since he left Montana to go to the West Coast." I had a special thought for my wife. To keep things straight with her, I thought, "I did not leave your brother. Your brother, who is a bastard, left me." All this, of course, was internal. For my mother-in-law I tried to think of the time she must have committed adultery. For both my wife and her mother, I thought, "The only thing the matter with the bastard is that all the antifreeze he poured into his radiator last night at Black Jack's has drained out."

It rained all the way back to Wolf Creek, and we were stuck in the gumbo all the way from the Elkhorn to Jim McGregor's ranch house, where the road turned to gravel. Of course, Ken drove the truck and Paul and I pushed. I pushed on an empty stomach. Just before I felt the sides of my stomach collapse, I went around to the driver's side of the cab, and asked, "Ken, how about getting your brother off his mattress to help us push?"

Ken said to me, "You know more about a truck than that. You know I have to have ballast in the rear end, or the rear wheels will just spin and not pull us out of the mud."

I went back to the rear end, and Paul and I pushed the ballast to the ranch house. It was just as hard pushing downhill as uphill. We might as well have been in eastern Montana pushing a half-ton truck plus ballast up the Powder River, where they invented gumbo.

When we reached Wolf Creek, Paul stayed to help me unload the truck, which was overweight with mud and water. We unloaded the mattress last. Then I started for bed, being all in, or maybe being just weak from hunger, and Paul left for Helena. On my way to my room I saw Neal and his mother at the front door. The ballast had put on two red-white-and-blue Davis Cup sweaters. He was lying to his mother who had caught him before he got all the way out. He was in the pink of condition. I knew of two grocery crates who would be glad to see him.

I went to bed and fought off sleep until I collected enough of my wits to come to a fairly obvious conclusion and to consolidate it into one sentence. "If I don't get out of my wife's home for a few days I am not going to have any wife left." So I telephoned my brother the next morning from the grocery store where no one at the house could hear. I asked him if he didn't have a little time coming yet from his summer vacation, because I needed to be at Seeley Lake for a while.

Seeley Lake is where we have our summer cabin. It is only seventeen miles from the Blackfoot Canyon and not much farther from the Swan, a river beautiful as its name as it floats by the Mission Glaciers. I think my brother still felt yesterday's rain running down his back, when no one moved to let us crawl under the tarp, so he understood what was on my mind. Anyway, he said, "I'll ask the boss."

That night I asked my wife a question—in dealing with her I had a better chance to dominate the situation by asking a question than by making a series of declarative sentences. So I asked my wife, "Don't you think it would be a good idea for Paul and me to spend a few days at Seeley Lake?" She looked right through me and said, "Yes."

I survived the next day and the day following, when Paul and I crossed the Continental Divide and left the world behind, so I thought. But the moment we started flowing into the Pacific, Paul began to tell me about a new girl he had picked up. I listened on my toes, ready to jump in any direction.

I was in the same old box. Maybe he was telling me something I wouldn't like but would dislike less if I heard it first as literature—or maybe I was wasting my time in being suspicious—maybe he was just my brother and a reporter passing on news items to me that were too personal or poetical to be published.

"She's kind of funny," he said, when it was clear we were coasting down the western slope of our continent. "Yes," he said, as though I had commented, "she's kind of funny. The only place she'll let you screw her is in the boys' locker room in the high school gymnasium."

What he said next sounded as if it also were in answer to something I had said, and maybe it was. "Oh, she's got that all figured out. She knows a window in the boys' toilet that's always unlocked and I push her up and then she reaches down and gives me a hand."

The next he said on his own. "She makes you screw her on the rubbing table."

I spent the rest of the way to Seeley Lake trying to figure out whether he was telling me he was in trouble with some dame or whether he was seeing to it that I kept enlarging my mental life even though I had gone off and married. I went on thinking until I noticed that I could smell witch hazel, rubbing alcohol, hot radiators with sweat clothes drying on them, and the insides of boys' lockers that wouldn't be cleaned out until the end of the football season.

I also thought, "It's damn hot right here now. The fishing isn't going to be much good. The fish will all be lying on the bottom." Then I tried to imagine a fish lying on its back on a rubbing table. It was hard to keep things fluid and not to fix on the picture of the fish helping the fisherman through the window in the toilet of the boys' locker room. About then we drove into the big tamaracks where our cabin is. There suddenly it was cool. The tamaracks are from eight to twelve hundred years old, their age and height keeping the heat out. We went swimming even before we unloaded the car.

After we had dressed but before we had combed our hair we carried out our swimming trunks and were hanging them on a clothes line that runs between two balsams. The line had been put up high where deer couldn't catch their horns in it, so I was standing on my toes trying to get a clothespin to stay when I heard a car turn off the Forest Service road into our lane.

My brother said, "Don't look around."

The car drove right up behind my back and stopped. Its engine panted in the heat. Even though it was panting in the curve of my back I didn't look around. Then somebody fell out of its front door.

When I looked, clothespin still in hand, I saw I had been in error in thinking somebody had fallen out of the front door of the car, because the car had no front door. It had floorboards, though, in the front, and on the floorboards sat a Hills Bros. coffee can, a bottle of 3–7–77, and an open bottle of strawberry pop. In Montana, we don't care whether the whiskey is much good if we can get strawberry pop for a chaser.

Just as if the scene had been taken for a Western film, it was high noon. My brother-in-law nodded in the driver's seat, as he probably had all the way from Wolf Creek.

Old Rawhide picked herself up out of the tamarack needles where she had fallen, took a look around to get reoriented, and then started walking straight for me. She would have walked through my brother if he hadn't reluctantly moved out of the way.

"Glad to meet you," she said to me, reaching out toward my hand that held the clothespin. Mechanically, I shifted the clothespin to the other hand, so she could shake the hand she was reaching for.

Sometimes a thing in front of you is so big you don't know whether to comprehend it by first getting a dim sense of the whole and then fitting in the pieces or by adding up the pieces until something calls out what it is. I put only a few pieces together before my voice called to me, "You'll never make your brother believe you didn't sucker him into this."

"How are you, anyway?" she asked. "I've brought Buster to go fishing with you."

She always called Neal "Buster." She had slept with so many men that the problem of remembering their names boggled her mind. By now all men besides Black Jack, Long Bow, and her two rodeo artists she called Buster, except me—me she just called "you." She could remember me but she could never remember that she had met me.

"Buster hasn't any money anymore," she said. "He needs your help."

Paul said to me, "Help him."

I asked, "How much money does he need?"

"We don't want your money," she said, "We want to go fishing with you."

She was drinking pink whiskey out of a pink paper cup. I went over to the car and asked the window next to the driver's seat, "Do you want to go fishing?"

Clearly, he had memorized a line in case he could not hear. He said, "I would like to go fishing with you and Paul."

I told him, "It's too hot to go fishing now." The dust was still drifting through the woods from the gravel turn-off to our lane.

He repeated, "I would like to go fishing with you and Paul."

Paul said, "Let's go."

I said to Paul, "Let's all get in our car, and I'll drive."

Paul said, "I'll drive," and I said, "OK."

Old Rawhide and Neal didn't like the idea of all of us going in our car. I think they wanted to be alone but they had become frightened or tired of being alone and wanted us somewhere around, though not in the front seat. Paul and I didn't argue. He got in the driver's seat and I sat next to him, and they mumbled to themselves. Finally, she started moving their stuff to our back seat—first the pink pop and then the red Hills Bros. coffee can.

I thought I noticed for the first time that they didn't have a fishing rod with them. If it had been anybody but Paul I would have asked him to hold it a minute while I checked to see if their rods had been left in their car, but for Paul the world of mercy did not include fishermen who left their tackle behind. He was tender to me and quick to offer them help, and would never kick about having to take them fishing at high noon while all the fish were lying at the bottom, but it would be just too damn bad for them if they didn't think enough about fishing to be able to fish when they got there.

They leaned on each other and slept. I was glad I did not have to drive—I had too many things to feel about. For instance, I felt about why women are such a bunch of suckers and how they all want to help some bastard like him—and not me. I felt an especially long time about why, when I tried to help somebody, I ended up offering him money or taking him fishing.

One steep grade and we were out of the pines and the

cool chain of lakes and into the glare of Blanchard Flats. Paul asked, "Which way do you want to turn when we get to the junction with the Blackfoot road?" "Up," I said. "The canyon is too rough water for them to fish. Let's turn up to the head of the canyon where there are some fine holes before the river goes into the cliffs." So we left the main road at the head of the flats and bumped over glacial remains until we came to a big fork in the river with Ponderosa pines beside it where we could park our car in the shade.

In the middle of the river where it had forked was a long sand bar. If you could wade out there, you had a perfect fishing spot. Big fish on either side of you, and no sunken logs or big roots or rocks to foul you up when you were landing them—just sand to skid them over so that they scarcely noticed they lay on land until they gasped for water.

Although I had fished this hole many times, I went to take another look at it before I put up my rod. I approached it step by step like an animal that has been shot at before. Once I had rushed down rod in hand to demolish a fish on the first cast and actually had made the first cast when part of the mountain on the other side started falling into the river. I had never seen the bear and he evidently had never seen me until he heard me swear when I was slow in reacting to the first strike. I didn't even know what the bear had been doing—fishing, swimming, drinking. All I know is that he led a landslide up the mountain.

If you have never seen a bear go over the mountain, you

have never seen the job reduced to its essentials. Of course, deer are faster, but not going straight uphill. Not even elk have the power in their hindquarters. Deer and elk zigzag and switchback and stop and pose while really catching their breath. The bear leaves the earth like a bolt of lightning retrieving itself and making its thunder backwards.

Paul had his rod up when I got back to the car. He asked me, "Are Neal and his friend coming?" I looked in the back of the car where they were still asleep, except that they stirred when I merely looked so maybe they weren't. I said, "Neal, wake up and tell us what you want to do." Much against his will, he made fitful efforts to wake up. Finally, he shed Old Rawhide off his shoulder and got out of the car stiffly, already an old man. Looking over the bank, he asked, "What about that hole?" I told him, "It's a good one. In fact, so are the next four or five."

"Can you wade out to the sand bar?" he asked, and I told him not usually but it had been so hot lately the river had dropped a foot or more and he shouldn't have any trouble.

"That's what I'll do, I'll stay here and fish," Neal said. He never once referred to her. Besides being devoted to the art of ignoring women, he also knew that Paul and I didn't think she should be here, so he may have thought if he didn't mention her we wouldn't notice her.

Old Rawhide woke up and handed Paul the bottle of 3-7-77. "Have a snort," she said. Paul took her hand and moved it around to where she was offering the drink to Neal. As I said, for several reasons, including our father,

Paul and I did not drink when we fished. Afterwards, yes, in fact, as soon as our wet clothes were off and we could stand on them instead of the pine needles one of us would reach for the glove compartment in the car where we always carried a bottle.

If you think what I am about to tell you next is a contradiction to this, then you will have to realize that in Montana drinking beer does not count as drinking.

Paul opened the trunk of our car and counted out eight bottles of beer. He said to Neal, "Four for you and four for us. We'll sink two of them in each of the next two holes for you. They'll make you forget the heat." He told them where we would bury the bottles and then he should have thought before he told them he would hide our beer in the two following holes where we would finish fishing on our way back from the cliffs.

What a beautiful world it was once. At least a river of it was. And it was almost mine and my family's and just a few others' who wouldn't steal beer. You could leave beer to cool in the river, and it would be so cold when you got back it wouldn't foam much. It would be a beer made in the next town if the town were ten thousand or over. So it was either Kessler Beer made in Helena or Highlander Beer made in Missoula that we left to cool in the Blackfoot River. What a wonderful world it was once when all the beer was not made in Milwaukee, Minneapolis, or St. Louis.

We covered the beer with rocks so it wouldn't wash away. Then we started walking downstream a fishing distance. It was so hot even Paul was in no great rush. Suddenly he interrupted the lethargy. "Some day," he

Grasshopper

Cork body painted with oil or enamel for appearance. Works better when fly gets scuffed up.

said, "Neal is going to find out about himself and he won't come back to Montana. He doesn't like Montana."

My only preparation for this remark was that I had seen him studying Neal's face when he was waking up. I said, "I know he doesn't like to fish. He just likes to tell women he likes to fish. It does something for him and the women. And for the fish, too," I added. "It makes them all feel better."

It was so hot we stopped and sat on a log. When we were silent we could hear the needles falling like dry leaves. Suddenly the needles stopped. "I should leave Montana," he said. "I should go to the West Coast."

I had thought that, too, but I asked, "Why?"

"Here," he said, "I cover local sports and personal items and the police blotter. I don't have anything to do. Here I will never have anything to do."

"Except fish and hunt," I told him.

"And get into trouble," he added.

I told him again, "I've told you before I think I could be of some help if you want to work for a big paper. Then maybe you could do your own stuff—special features, even some day your own column."

It was so hot that the mirages on the river melted into each other. It was hard to know whether the utterances I had heard were delphic. He said, "Jesus, it's hot. Let's hit the river and cool off."

He stood and picked up his rod, and his beautiful silk-wrapped rod shimmered like the air around it. "I'll never leave Montana," he said. "Let's go fishing."

As we separated he said, "And I like the trouble that goes with it." So we were back to where we had started, and it was so hot the fishing just couldn't be any good.

And it wasn't. In the middle of a heat spell death comes to running water at high noon. You cast and cast on top of it, and nothing comes up out of it. Not even frogs jump. You begin to think you are the only moving thing in it. Maybe in the evolutionary process all life migrated from water to dry land, all except you and you are on the way with the part of you not in the water parching in the unaccustomed air. With the sun bouncing back at you from the water and hitting under your eyebrows, even your hat doesn't do any good.

I knew it was going to be tough before I started, so I tried to be extra sharp. I fished in front and back of big rocks where the fish could be in the shade and the water would bring them food without their having to work for it. I concentrated, too, on the water that slid under bushes where the fish could lie in the shade and wait for insects to hatch in the limbs and drop before them. There was nothing in the shade but shadows.

On the assumption that if an idea doesn't produce anything at all, then the opposite might work, I gave up shade entirely and walked into the open meadow that was crackling with grasshoppers. To one familiar with a subject, there is no trouble to find reasons for the opposite idea. I said to myself, "It is summer and the grasshoppers are out in the sun and the fish will be, too." I put on a cork-bellied fly that looked like one of those big, juicy, yellow hoppers. I fished close to shore where even big fish wait for grasshoppers to make one mistake. After fishing with the floating cork grasshopper, I put on a big fly with a yellow wool body that would absorb water and sink like a dead grasshopper. Still, not even a frog jumped.

The brain gives up a lot less easily than the body, so fly fishermen have developed what they call the "curiosity theory," which is about what it says it is. It is the theory that fish, like men, will sometimes strike at things just to find out what they are and not because they look good to eat. With most fly fishermen, it is the "last resort theory," but it sometimes almost works. I put on a fly that George Croonenberghs had tied for me when he was a kid and several decades before he became one of the finest fly tyers of the West. This fly, tied in a moment of juvenile enthusiasm, had about everything on it from deer hair to fool-hen feathers.

Once when I was fishing on the upper Blackfoot I saw a strange thing with a neck and head being washed downstream while trying to swim straight across. I couldn't figure out what it was until it landed and shook itself. Then I recognized that it was a bobcat, and, in case you don't know what a wet bobcat looks like, it looks like a little wet cat. While this one was wet, it was a skinny, meek little thing, but after it got dry and fluffy again and felt sure that it was a cat once more, it turned around, took a look at me, and hissed.

I hope my old fishing pal, George Croonenberghs, doesn't mind my saying that this juvenile creation of his struggling in the water looked something like the bobcat. Anyway, it looked like something interesting to a fish.

Out of the lifeless and hopeless depths, life appeared. He came so slowly it seemed as if he and history were being made on the way. After a while he got to be ten inches long. He came closer and closer, but beyond a certain point he never got any bigger, so I guess that's how big he was. At what seemed a safe distance, the ten-incher began to circle George's Bobcat Special. I have never seen such large disbelieving eyes in such a little fish. He kept his eyes always on the fly and seemed to let the water circle him around it. Then he turned himself over to gravity and slowly sank. When he got to be about a six-incher he reversed himself and became a ten-incher again to give George's fly a final inspection. Halfway round the circle he took his eye off the fly and saw me and darted out of sight. This undoubtedly is the only time that a fish ever seriously studied George's juvenile creation, although I still carry it with me for sentimental reasons.

I abandoned the curiosity theory, got down on my belly and had a drink of water and was thirstier when I finished. I began to think of that beer, and of quitting this waste of time. In fact, I would have quit and sat in the shade, except that I didn't want to be sitting in the shade when my brother asked, "How many did you get?" and I had to answer, "I went for the horse collar." So I said to myself prayerfully, "I'll try one more hole."

I don't like to pray and not have my prayers come true, so I walked a long way on the bank looking for this last prayerful hole. When I saw it, actually I wasn't looking hard because it was an ordinary piece of water, but when I took a sudden second look I could see that fish were jumping all over it. Almost at the same moment I smelled something, and it smelled bad. In fact, on a hot day it smelled very bad. I didn't want to get any closer, but hitherto nonexistent fish were jumping right in front of me. I circled the dead beaver halfway down the bank and made for the water. I knew I was set.

When I saw the dead beaver I knew why the fish were jumping. Even a weekend fisherman would know that the dead beaver had drawn a swarm of bees that were flying low over the ground and water. Being my kind of fisherman, I knew I had the right fly to match them, and I did not think that my brother would. He didn't carry many flies—they were all in his hat band, twenty or twenty-five at the most, but really only four or five kinds, since each one was in several sizes. They were what fishermen call "generals," each a fly with which a skillful fisherman can imitate a good many insects and in different stages from larval to winged. My brother felt about flies much the way my father, who was a fine carpenter, felt about tools—he maintained anybody could make a showing as a carpenter if he had enough tools. But I wasn't a good enough fisherman to be disdainful of tools. I carried a box-ful of flies, the "generals" and also what fishermen call the "specials"—flies that imitate a very specific hatch, such as flying ants, mayflies, stone flies, spruce bugs. And bees.

I took a fly out of my box that George Croonenberghs had tied to imitate a bee. It didn't look much like a bee. If you are starting to be a fly fisherman you better be careful not to confuse yourself with the fish and buy "counter flies"—flies that in a drugstore counter look to you like the insect they are named after. George had a glass tank in his backyard which he filled with water. Then he would lie under it and study the insect he was going to imitate floating on top where it doesn't look like an insect anywhere else. I put on George's Bee that did not look like a bee, and caught three just like that. They were nice-sized but not big—fourteen inches or so. Still, I was grateful to get the horse collar off my neck.

Somehow it's hard to quit with an odd number of fish, so I wanted one more for four, but I had to work hard to get him. When I finally did, he was small and I knew that he was the last and that the rest had got wise to George's Bee. The increasing heat of the afternoon had the opposite effect on the dead beaver and he gathered strength, so I climbed the bank and walked into the wind to the next bend where I could sit and look downstream for Paul. Now he could ask me, and I wouldn't be ashamed to be caught sitting in the shade.

I sat there in the hot afternoon trying to forget the beaver and trying to think of the beer. Trying to forget the beaver, I also tried to forget my brother-in-law and Old Rawhide. I knew I was going to have a long time to sit here and forget, because my brother would never quit with three or four fish, as I had, and even he was going to have a hard time getting more. I sat there and forgot and forgot, until what remained was the river that went by and I who watched. On the river the heat mirages danced with each other and then they danced through each other and then they joined hands and danced around each other. Eventually the watcher joined the river, and there was only one of us. I believe it was the river.

Even the anatomy of a river was laid bare. Not far downstream was a dry channel where the river had run once, and part of the way to come to know a thing is through its death. But years ago I had known the river when it flowed through this now dry channel, so I could enliven its stony remains with the waters of memory.

In death it had its pattern, and we can only hope for as much. Its overall pattern was the favorite serpentine curve of the artist sketched on the valley from my hill to the last hill I could see on the other side. But internally it was made of sharp angles. It ran seemingly straight for a while, turned abruptly, then ran smoothly again, then met another obstacle, again was turned sharply and again ran smoothly. Straight lines that couldn't be exactly straight and angles that couldn't have been exactly right angles became the artist's most beautiful curve and swept from here across the valley to where it could be no longer seen.

I also became the river by knowing how it was made. The Big Blackfoot is a new glacial river that runs and drops fast. The river is a straight rapids until it strikes big rocks or big trees with big roots. This is the turn that is not exactly at right angles. Then it swirls and deepens among big rocks and circles back through them where big fish live under the foam. As it slows, the sand and small rocks it picked up in the fast rapids above begin to settle out and are deposited, and the water becomes shallow and quiet. After the deposit is completed, it starts running again.

On a hot afternoon the mind can also create fish and arrange them according to the way it has just made the river. It will have the fish spend most of their time in the "big blue" at the turn, where they can lie protected by big rocks and take it easy and have food washed to them by big waters. From there, they can move into the fast rapids above when they are really hungry or it is September and cool, but it is hard work living in such fast water all the time. The mind that arranges can also direct the fish into the quiet water in the evening when gnats and small moths come out. Here the fisherman should be told to use his small dry flies and to wax them so they will float. He should also be informed that in quiet evening water everything must be perfect because, with the glare from the sun gone, the fish can see everything, so even a few hairs too many in the tail of the fly can make all the difference. The mind can make all these arrangements, but of course the fish do not always observe them.

Fishermen also think of the river as having been made with them partly in mind, and they talk of it as if it had been. They speak of the three parts as a unity and call it "a hole," and the fast rapids they call "the head of the hole" and the big turn they call "the deep blue" or "pool" and the quiet, shallow water below they call "the tail of the hole," which they think is shallow and quiet so that they can have a place to wade across and "try the other side."

As the heat mirages on the river in front of me danced with and through each other, I could feel patterns from my own life joining with them. It was here, while waiting for my brother, that I started this story, although, of course, at the time I did not know that stories of life are often more like rivers than books. But I knew a story had begun, perhaps long ago near the sound of water. And I sensed that ahead I would meet something that would never erode so there would be a sharp turn, deep circles, a deposit, and quietness.

The fisherman even has a phrase to describe what he does when he studies the patterns of a river. He says he is "reading the water," and perhaps to tell his stories he has to do much the same thing. Then one of his biggest problems is to guess where and at what time of day life lies ready to be taken as a joke. And to guess whether it is going to be a little or a big joke.

For all of us, though, it is much easier to read the waters of tragedy.

"Did you do any good?" The voice and the question suggested that if I woke up and looked around I would see my brother. The suggestion became a certainty when the voice asked, "What the hell are you doing here?"

"Oh, just thinking," I answered, as we all answer when we don't know what we have been doing.

He said it was too hot to fish but he had fished until he caught "a fairly good mess," which meant ten or twelve and just fair-sized. "Let's go and get that beer," he said. When he said "beer," everything else came back to me—the beer, the beaver, the brother-in-law, and his fishing companion.

"God, let's get that beer," I said.

Paul kept spinning a bottle opener around his little finger. We were so dry that we could feel in our ears that we were trying to swallow. For talk, we only repeated the lyric refrain of the summer fisherman, "A bottle of beer would sure taste good."

A game trail cut from the bank to the river where we

had left the beer for ourselves, and we went down it stiff-legged. Paul was ahead, and when he got near the bottom he loosened his knees and made for the river. We had buried the beer in moving water to keep it cool but not where the water was so fast it would wash the beer downstream.

"I can't see it," he said, feeling with his feet. "Oh," I said, "you just haven't found the right place. It has to be there." And I waded out to find it for him, already having doubts that I could.

He said, "There's no use looking around. That's where we buried it." He pointed to holes in the clay of the bottom where we had pulled out rocks to cover the bottles. I felt in one of the holes with the toe of my wading boot as if a bottle of beer might have escaped my attention in a hole the size of a small rock. He was doing the same thing. There were no bottles of beer hiding in holes too small for a bottle to get into.

We had been saving our thirst for a long time. Now knee-deep by the holes in the clay bottom, we cupped our hands and started drinking out of the river. Between us and the car there were still three more holes where we had buried the beer, but we had about quit hoping for beer.

Paul said, "All told, we buried eight bottles of beer in four holes. Do you think they could have drunk eight bottles of beer, besides the rest of that 3–7–77?"

He was being gentle, for my sake and for the sake of my wife and my mother-in-law. But I couldn't argue against anything he was thinking. Although we had walked back on the trail, we were always in sight of the river and

The Can of Worms

neither of us had seen a fisherman. Who else could have taken it?

I said, "Paul, I'm sorry. I wish I knew how I could have stayed away from this guy."

"You couldn't," he said.

Suddenly we did something that for a time seemed strange to me, given the fact that we knew without hurrying to look that all the beer was gone and that we also knew without evidence who had taken it. Suddenly we turned and came out of that water with a roar, like two animals as they finish fording a river, making jumps when the water gets shallower and bringing waves to shore long after they get there. Later, I could see easily that our being gentle was for each other and the roar and the jumps to the shore were for those who had taken our beer.

The rocks rattled and leaped out of our way as we walked along the shore. In each of the next three holes we enacted the rite of staring at the emptiness of stones that have been rolled aside.

We came then to where in the distance we could see our car on the bank and where below the river forked with a sandbar in between.

Nobody had moved the car to keep it in the shade. I could feel how hot it would be if we rubbed against a fender while shedding our wet clothes.

I said, "I don't see them." "I don't either," Paul said. "They can't be in the car," I said. He added, "Today a dog would die in a car if he were left in it."

Walking fast and watching for them, I wasn't watching where I was going and stumbled over a rock and lit on my elbow which I had stuck out to avoid falling on my rod. I was picking the grit out of my cut when Paul said, "What's on the sandbar?" Still trying to pick the blue-black specks out of my bruise, I said, "Maybe it's the bear."

"What bear?" he asked.

"The bear that went over the mountain," I told him. "That's where he comes down the mountain to drink."

"That's no bear," he said.

I studied the sandbar. "Maybe it's two bears," I suggested.

"It's two, all right," he said, "but it's not bears."

"Why do you keep saying 'it' when it's two?" I asked him.

"It's not bears," he said. "It's red."

"Wait until you see it go up the mountain," I told him. "Then you'll see it's bears. Bears go straight up a mountain."

We were walking very slowly now, as if ready to jump sideways if it moved suddenly.

"It's red," he said, "and it's whatever drank our beer."

I told him, "It isn't even human. It's red as you say."

By now, we had come to an uneasy stop, like animals approaching a waterhole and seeing something in the water where they were going to drink. We didn't snort or paw, but we could feel what it would be like to snort and paw. We had no choice but to go ahead.

We kept going until we knew, but couldn't believe it. "Bear, hell," Paul said. "It's a bare ass."

"Two bare asses," I said.

"That's what I meant," he said. "It's two bare asses. Both are red."

We kept not believing after we knew. "I'll be a son of a bitch," Paul said. "Me, too," I said to confirm it.

You have never really seen an ass until you have seen two sunburned asses on a sandbar in the middle of a river. Nearly all the rest of the body seems to have evaporated. The body is a large red ass about to blister, with hair on one end of it for a head and feet attached to the other end for legs. By tonight, it will run a fever.

That's the way it looked then, but, when I view it now through the sentimentality of memory, it belongs to a pastoral world where you could take off your clothes, screw a dame in the middle of the river, then roll over on your belly and go to sleep for a couple of hours.

If you tried something like that on the Blackfoot River these days, half the city of Great Falls would be standing on the shore waiting to steal your clothes when you went to sleep. Maybe sooner.

"Hey," Paul yelled with a hand on each side of his mouth. Then he blasted a whistle with a finger from each hand.

"Do you think they are all right?" he asked me. "You used to work every summer in the sun in the Forest Service."

"Well," I told him, "I never knew anybody who died of sunburn, but they sure as hell aren't going to wear any wool underwear for a couple of weeks."

"Let's get them to the car," he said. We took off our baskets and leaned our rods against a log so they could be seen and nobody would step on them.

We had waded almost to the sandbar when Paul stopped and barred me with his arm. "Just a minute," he said. "I want to take another look so I'll always remember."

We stood there for a minute and made an engraving on what little was left of the blank tablets of our minds. It was an engraving in color. In the foreground of the engraving was a red Hills Bros. coffee can, then red tenderized soles of feet pointing downward, two red asses sizzling under the solar system, and in the background a pile of clothes with her red panties on top. To the side were the remains of the 3–7–77, red hot when touched. There was no fishing rod or basket in sight.

Paul said, "May he get three doses of clap, and may he recover from all but the first."

I never again threw a line in this hole, which I came to regard as a kind of wild game sanctuary.

We waded the rest of the way to the sandbar without splashing, fearful of waking them. I think we thought, "When they wake up they will start peeling." I know what I thought. I had worked several summers in rattlesnake country in late August, and I thought when they wake up and find out how hot it is they will shed their skins and be blind for a while and strike at anything they hear. I can remember I kept thinking, they will be very dangerous when they wake up, so I walked around them warily, staying beyond striking distance.

When we got close to them, they developed anatomical parts that couldn't be seen from shore. They developed legs between their asses and their feet, and they sprouted backs and necks, especially necks, between their asses and their hair. It was red into their hair, which was curly. It was hard to know whether their hair was naturally curly or whether it had frizzled in the sun. Each hair was distinct and could have been made with a hot curling iron.

Paul had gone over to see what was left in the bottle of 3-7-77, but I stayed to study the anatomy. Each hair was sore at its root, but that's not what I backed off to tell Paul. I was so studious I backed off until I bumped into him.

"She's got a tattoo on her ass," I told him.

"No kidding," he said.

He circled her as if to get on the downwind side of big game before trying to approach it. Then he backed off and completed the circle back to me.

"What are the initials of her cowboys?" he asked. "B. I. and B. L.," I told him.

He said, "Are you sure?"

I said, "Sure, I'm sure."

"Well," he said, "they don't fit, because she has LO tattooed on one cheek of her ass and VE on the other."

I told him, "LOVE spells love, with a hash-mark between."

"I'll be damned," he said, and backed away, circled around and started to study the situation all over again.

She jumped straight up like a barber pole. She was red, white, and blue. She was white where she had been lying on her belly in the sand, and her back completed the patriotic color scheme, red into her hair except for the blue-black tattoo. Somebody should have spun her around and played "The Stars and Stripes Forever."

She looked wildly about her to get oriented, and then

streaked for the clothes pile and pulled on her red panties. When she was sure you couldn't look without paying at the part that made her living, she relaxed. She didn't put on any more clothes, but came sauntering back, took one look at me, and said, "Oh, it's you."

Then she looked at both of us, and said, "Well, what's on your mind, boys?" She was ready to entertain company.

I said, "We came out to get Neal."

She was disappointed. "Oh," she said, "you mean Buster."

I said, "I mean him," and when I pointed at him he groaned. I think he did not want to wake up and find out about his sunburn and hangover. He groaned again and sank even deeper into the sand. Her white belly was covered with sand, and had creases in it where her skin had folded over when she was lying on it. Sand ran out of her navel.

Paul said, "Get your clothes on and help us with him." She looked indignant. She said, "I can take care of him." Paul said, "You already have."

She said, "He's my man. I can take care of him. The sun doesn't bother me." And I suppose she was right—it's under the sun where a fisherman's whore makes her money.

Paul said, "Get your clothes on or I'll kick you in the ass." Both she and I knew he meant it.

Paul went over to the clothes pile and started separating out Neal's clothes from hers. They were in the order in which they had come off. That's why her red pants were on top of the pile, and her belt on the bottom.

I said to Paul, "That's a good thing to do, but we can't put any clothes on him. I don't think he can stand their touch."

"We'll take him home naked, then," Paul said.

When Neal heard the word "home" he sat up so suddenly that the sand ran off him in streams.

"I don't want to go home," he said.

"Where do you want to go, Neal?" I asked. "I don't know," he said, "but I don't want to go home."

I told him, "There are three women there who know how to take care of you."

"I don't want to see three women," he said, and more sand ran off him.

Old Rawhide held her clothes under one arm. I reached down, picked up Neal's clothes, and put them under his arm. "Here," I said, taking his other arm, "I'll help you wade back to shore."

He jumped away in pain. "Don't touch me," he said. To Old Rawhide he said, "You carry my clothes. They hurt when I hold them."

"You take them," she said to me, and I did, and she took Neal by the arm he had pulled away from me and led him to the edge of the water. Part way out, she turned around and said to me, "He's my man." She was a strong woman and very tough. The Blackfoot is a big river and hard to wade. The man couldn't have made it without the strength in her legs.

Part way across Paul turned around and went back for what was left of the bottle of 3–7–77. After Old Rawhide got Neal all the way across she left him feeling his way through the rocks with his tenderized feet, and waded back to the sandbar. Her feet were tenderized, too, but she waded back to the sandbar to get the Hills Bros. coffee can.

I met her on the shore when she returned.

"What's good about the coffee can?" I asked her.

"I don't know," she said. "But Buster always likes to have it with him."

There was a light blanket on the back seat of the car that we used to spread on the ground when we were going to have a picnic. Fir needles had stuck on it. We put Neal and Old Rawhide in the back seat and threw the light blanket over them—probably for several reasons. Probably to keep them from getting further burned, especially by the wind, and probably also so the state police wouldn't arrest us for indecent exposure. But the moment the blanket touched their shoulders, they writhed until it fell off. So we drove to Wolf Creek, completely exposed to the elements and the police.

Neal never sat up straight, but he murmured from time to time, "I don't want to see three women." Each time he murmured this, Old Rawhide would sit up straight and say, "Don't worry. I'm your woman. I'll take care of you." I was driving. Each time he murmured this, I took a firm grip on the wheel. I didn't want to see three women either.

For most of the trip Paul and I didn't speak to each other or to them. We just let one murmur through his armpit and the other jump up straight and then recede into the clothes pile. But as we neared Wolf Creek I could feel Paul getting ready to change the format. Slowly his body shifted until he could reach to the back seat. A murmur came again, "I don't want to go home." Paul reached and grabbed the arm that belonged to the armpit, and pulled him up. The arm turned white, even when it was sunburned. "You're almost home," Paul said. "There's no other place you can go." There were no more murmurs. Paul kept holding the arm.

The whore was still tough, and she and Paul got into a big argument. Paul was used to talking to tough women and she was used to tough talk. The argument was over whether we were going to dump her as soon as we got to town or whether she was going to stay and take care of Buster. Mostly what was said was, "God damn you, I am," and "God damn you, you're not." He said to me, as part of the argument, "When you get to town, stop at the log dance hall."

The log dance hall was the first building at the edge of town. It was a good place to have fights, and there had been plenty of them there, especially on Saturday nights —every time some home-town drunk from Wolf Creek tried to dance with the girl of some drunk who had come from the Dearborn country.

You couldn't tell by the profanity who was winning the argument, but as we got closer to town she would reach into the clothes pile and put some of it on her. There is a bend in the creek and the road just before you get to the log dance hall. When she saw the bend, she realized she wouldn't have all her clothes on by the time we reached the dance hall, so she scurried through the pile grabbing the rest that belonged to her.

Just as I stopped the car, she made one wild grab into the pile, opened the door of the car and jumped out. She was on the opposite side of the car from Paul, and must have figured that would give her a big enough head start. She left the back door swinging and took a good hold on the clothes in her arms. At the top of the clothes in her arms was Neal's underwear, which she had taken either by accident or for a keepsake. She made one more grunt as she tightened her hold on her belongings, like a packer throwing a double diamond hitch just to be sure the whole load will stick together on the rough trip ahead.

Then she said to my brother, "You stinking bastard."

Paul came out of that car as if the body of it had fallen off, and took after her.

I think I knew how he felt. Much as he hated her, he really had no strong feeling about her. It was the bastard in the back seat without any underwear that he hated. The bastard who had ruined most of our summer fishing. The bait-fishing bastard. The bait-fishing bastard who had violated everything that our father had taught us about fishing by bringing a whore and a coffee can of worms but not a rod. The bait-fishing bastard who had screwed his whore in the middle of our family river. And after drinking our beer. The bastard right in the back of the car who was untouchable because of three Scotch women.

She was running barefoot and trying to hang on to the rest of her clothes and his underwear, so Paul caught up to her in about ten jumps. On the run he kicked her, I think, right where the "LO" and the "VE" came together. For

George's Bobcat Special

*This fly was a prototype that failed. Made
on orange-painted cork with ten grey-and-ginger
hackle tips tied to the head in a fan
shape—looks more like a feather duster.
A floating salmonfly in distress.*

several seconds both of her feet trailed behind her in the air. It was to become a frozen moment of memory.

When I could move, I took two quick looks at my brother-in-law, and counted to four. The four was for those four women in the street ready to protect him—one in the middle of the street and three in a house part way down it.

Suddenly, I developed a passion to kick a woman in the ass. I was never aware of such a passion before, but now it overcame me. I jumped out of the car, and caught up to her, but she had been kicked in the ass before and by experts, so I missed her completely. Still, I felt better for the effort.

Paul and I stood together and watched her high-tail it down the road through town. She had no choice. She lived on the other side of a town which is in a narrow gulch. After she got near home, she stopped several times to look back, and Paul and I didn't like what we couldn't hear she was saying. Each of these times we pretended that we were going to start after her again, and she edged closer to her shack. Finally, she and her clothes pile disappeared, and we were left with the back seat. "Now we haven't anything left to do but take him home," my brother said. As we walked back to the car, he added, "You're in trouble." "I know, I know," I said. But I didn't really know. I still didn't know what Scottish women look like when they struggle to keep their pride and haven't much reason left to keep it. In case you have any doubts, they keep it.

Even Neal tried to pull himself together. He tried to

put on some clothes before the women saw him. He piled his clothes outside the car, and, when he couldn't find his underwear, he started trying to get into his pants, but he stumbled and kept stumbling. He held his pants out in front of him and tried to catch up to them. He was stumbling so fast he was running after them, but he never got any closer to them than an arm's length.

He was breathless when we caught him and he gasped when we put on his pants. His feet were too swollen for shoes. We put his shirt over his shoulders with its tails hanging out. When we brought him into the house, he looked like something shipwrecked we had found on an island.

Florence came out of the kitchen and when she saw what Paul and I had, she began drying her hands on her dish towel.

"What have you done to my boy?" she asked the brothers who were holding him up.

Jessie then followed from the kitchen when she heard her mother. She was tall and red-headed anyway, and I was shrunken before her from trying to hold up her brother.

"You bastard," she said to me. The bastard I was holding weighed a ton.

"No," Paul said.

"Get out of the way," I told her. "We have to put him to bed."

"He's badly sunburned," Paul said.

The women I was brought up with never stood around trying on different life styles when there was something to be done, especially something medical. Most people have an immediate chemical reaction to shrink from pain or disfigurement, but the women I was brought up with were magnetized by the medical.

"Let's get him undressed," Florence said, backing to the bedroom door and holding it open.

"I'll find Dotty," Jessie said. Dotty was the registered nurse.

Neal didn't want his mother to undress him and his mother thought we were clumsy and kept pushing us away. Before a situation could develop, Jessie was in the bedroom with Dorothy. I didn't know how a nurse could get into a uniform so fast, but I could hear the swish of starch as she came through the door. When Neal heard the starch, he stopped wriggling away from us. Dorothy was short and powerful and Jessie and her mother were tall and skinny, but strong. Paul and I stood by the bed wondering why we hadn't been able to get off a pair of pants and a shirt. In an instant he was a red carcass on a white sheet.

In almost the same instant Paul and I, who held the world in our hands when we held a four-and-a-half-ounce fishing rod, were not even orderlies. We were left to one side as if we couldn't warm water or find a bandage or bring it in if we found it.

The first time Jessie passed me she made a point of saying, "Get out of the way." I knew she hadn't liked it when I had said it to her.

By chemical reaction, Paul and I backed for the bedroom door, but he beat me to it and was on his way to

Black Jack's for a drink, which I needed, too. I didn't get the bedroom door closed, though, before I was to be visited by three women.

As soon as Florence saw her boy in red she came close to knowing what the score was. With Scottish women, the medical barely precedes the moral. She took another look to make sure that Dorothy had taken charge, and then she called to me.

She stood in front of me as rigid as if she were posing for the nineteenth-century Scottish photographer David Octavius Hill. Her head might have been held for the slow exposure by an unseen rod behind her neck. "Tell me," she said, "how does it happen that he is burned from head to foot?"

I wasn't going to tell her, and I wasn't going to lie if for no reason other than that I knew I couldn't get away with it. I had long ago learned, sometimes to my sorrow, that Scottish piety is accompanied by a complete foreknowledge of sin. That's what we mean by original sin—we don't have to do it to know about it.

I told her, "He didn't feel like going fishing with us, and when we got back he was lying asleep in the sand."

She knew I wasn't going to go beyond that. Finally the nineteenth-century photographer released her neck from the brace. "I love you," she said, and I knew she couldn't think of anything else to say. I also knew she meant it. "Why don't you get out of here?" she added.

"Wait," Dorothy said to me, and turned her job over to Florence. Dorothy and I were the ones who had married into the family and often had the feeling that if we didn't hang together we would be strung up separately. "Don't worry about him," she said. "Second-degree burn. Blisters. Peeling. Fever. A couple of weeks. Don't worry about him. Don't worry about us. We women can handle it.

"In fact," she said, "why don't you and Paul get out of here? We have Ken and he can do anything and Neal is his brother.

"Besides," she said, "I think you aren't even wanted here. All you can do is stand around and watch, and right now nobody in the family wants to be watched."

Although she was short, she had big hands. She took one of mine in one of hers, and put on the pressure. I thought that was her good-bye and turned to go, but she pulled me back and gave me a fast kiss and was on the job again.

It seemed as if the women had agreed on some kind of a shuttle system whereby two were always working on Neal and one on me. "Wait," Jessie said, before I had closed the door behind me.

A man is at a disadvantage talking to a woman as tall as he is, and I had tried long and hard to overcome this handicap.

"You don't like him, do you?" she asked.

"Woman," I asked, "can't I love you without liking him?"

She just stood looking at me, so I went on talking and saying more than I had intended. I said things she already knew, but possibly one thing she wanted to hear again. "Jessie," I said, "you know I don't know any card tricks.

I don't like him. I never will. But I love you. Don't keep testing me, though, by giving me no choices. Jessie, don't let him..." I stopped from going on because I knew I should have found a shorter way to say what I had already said.

"Don't let him what?" she asked. "What were you going to say?"

"I can't remember what I was going to say," I replied, "except that I feel I have lost touch with you."

"I am trying to help someone," she said. "Someone in my family. Don't you understand?"

I said, "I should understand."

"I am not able to help," she said.

"I should understand that, too," I said.

"We are talking too long," she said. "Why don't you and Paul go back to the Blackfoot and finish your fishing trip? You're no help here. But wherever you go, never lose touch with me."

Although she said we had talked too long, she took only one backward step. "Tell me," she asked, "why is he burned from head to foot?" When it comes to asking questions, Scottish daughters are almost complete recapitulations of their mothers.

I told her what I had told her mother, and she looked like her mother while she listened.

"Tell me," she said, "just before you brought Neal in, did you happen to see the whore run through town with an armful of clothes?"

"At a distance," I told her.

"Tell me," she asked, "if my brother comes back next summer, will you try to help me help him?"

It took a long time to say it, but I said it. I said, "I will try."

Then she said, "He won't come back." Then she added, "Tell me, why is it that people who want help do better without it—at least, no worse. Actually, that's what it is, no worse. They take all the help they can get, and are just the same as they always have been."

"Except that they are sunburned," I said.

"That's no different," she said.

"Tell me," I asked her, "if your brother comes back next summer, will we both try to help him?"

"If he comes back," she nodded. I thought I saw tears in her eyes but I was mistaken. In all my life, I was never to see her cry. And also he was never to come back.

Without interrupting each other, we both said at the same time, "Let's never get out of touch with each other." And we never have, although her death has come between us.

She said, "Get out of the way," only this time she smiled when she said it. Then she started closing the door in my face. When there was only a crack left, we kissed, and with one eye I tried to look around her. They had him greased from head to foot like a roasting ear of corn. They had enough bandages open to go on from there and wrap him up for a mummy.

I went down to Black Jack's and had a drink with Paul, and then we had another. He insisted on paying for both and on going back to the Blackfoot that night. He said, "I asked for a couple of days off, so I have another day coming." Then he insisted we go by way of Missoula and spend the night with father and mother. "Maybe," he said, "we can get the old man to go fishing with us tomorrow." Then he insisted on driving.

Our customary roles had been reversed, and I was the brother who was being taken fishing for the healing effects of cool waters. He knew I was being blamed for Neal, and he may well have thought my marriage was breaking up. He had heard me called a bastard, and he was out of the house when I and the three Scottish women publicly declared our love for each other, given the restrictions Scots put on such public declarations. Actually, I was feeling lordly with love and several times broke into laughter that I can't explain otherwise, but he could have thought I was trying to be brave about having made a mess of my life. I don't really know what he thought, but he was as tender as I usually tried to be to him.

On the way he said, "Mother will be glad to see us, too. But she gets excited when we show up without telling her ahead of time, so let's stop at Lincoln and telephone."

"You call her," I said. "She loves to hear you."

"Fine," he said, "but you ask father to come fishing with us."

So he made the arrangements for what turned out to be our last fishing trip together. He thought of all of us.

Even though we telephoned, Mother was excited when we got to Missoula. She tried to wring her hands in her apron, hug Paul, and laugh, all at the same time. Father stood in the background and just laughed. I still felt lordly and I just stood in the background. Whenever we had a family reunion, Mother and Paul were always the central attraction. He would lean back when he hugged her and laugh, but the best she could do was to hug and try to laugh.

It was late when we arrived in Missoula. We had been careful not to eat on the way, although there is a good restaurant in Lincoln, because we knew that, if we ate there, we would have to eat all over again in Missoula. Early in the dinner, Mother was especially nice to me, since she hadn't paid much attention to me so far, but soon she was back with fresh rolls, and she buttered Paul's.

"Here is your favorite chokecherry jelly," she said, passing it to him. She was a fine cook of wild berries and wild game, and she always had chokecherry jelly waiting for him. Somewhere along the line she had forgotten that it was I who liked chokecherry jelly, a gentle confusion that none of her men minded.

My father and mother were in retirement now, and neither one liked "being out of things," especially my mother, who was younger than my father and was used to "running the church." To them, Paul was the reporter, their chief contact with reality, the recorder of the world that was leaving them and that they had never known very well anyway. He had to tell them story after story, even though they did not approve of some of them. We sat around the table a long time. As we started to get up, I said to Father, "We'd appreciate it if you would go fishing with us tomorrow."

"Oh," my father said and sat down again, automatically unfolded his napkin, and asked, "Are you sure, Paul, that you want me? I can't fish some of those big holes anymore. I can't wade anymore."

Paul said, "Sure I want you. Whenever you can get near fish, you can catch them."

To my father, the highest commandment was to do whatever his sons wanted him to do, especially if it meant to go fishing. The minister looked as if his congregation had just asked him to come back and preach his farewell sermon over again.

It was getting to be after their bedtime, and it had been a long day for Paul and me, so I thought I'd help Mother with the dishes and then we'd turn in for the night. But I really knew that things weren't going to be that simple, and they knew it, too. Paul gave himself a stretch as soon as it was not immediately after dinner, and said, "I think I'll run over town and see some old pals. I'll be back before long, but don't wait up for me."

I helped my mother with the dishes. Although only one had left, all the voices had gone. He had stayed long enough after dinner for us to think he would be happy spending an evening at home. Each of us knew some of his friends, and all of us knew his favorite pal, who was big and easy and nice to us, especially to Mother. He had just got out of prison. His second stretch.

From the time my mother stood looking at the closed doors until she went to bed, she said only, "Goodnight." She said it over her shoulder near the head of the stairs to both my father and me.

I never could tell how much my father knew about my brother. I generally assumed that he knew a good deal because there is a substantial minority in every church congregation who regard it as their Christian duty to

Yellow Quill

Underwater drift during yellow stone fly hatch. Smaller sizes match a number of other hatches.

keep the preacher informed about the preacher's kids. Also, at times, my father would start to talk to me about Paul as if he were going to open up a new subject and then he would suddenly put a lid on it before the subject spilled out.

"Did you hear what Paul did lately?" he asked.

I told him, "I don't understand you. I hear all kinds of things about Paul. Mostly, I hear he's a fine reporter and a fine fisherman."

"No, no," my father said. "But haven't you heard what he does afterwards?"

I shook my head.

Then I think he had another thought about what he was thinking, and swerved from what he was going to say. "Haven't you heard," he asked me, "that he has changed his spelling of our name from Maclean to MacLean. Now he spells it with a capital L."

"Oh, sure," I said. "I knew all about that. He told me he got tired of nobody spelling his name right. They even wrote his paychecks with a capital L, so he finally decided to give up and spell his name the way others do."

My father shook his head at my explanation, its truth being irrelevant. He murmured both to himself and to me, "It's a terrible thing to spell our name with a capital L. Now somebody will think we are Scottish Lowlanders and not Islanders."

He went to the door and looked out and when he came back he didn't ask me any questions. He tried to tell me. He spoke in the abstract, but he had spent his life fitting abstractions to listeners so that listeners would have no trouble fitting his abstractions to the particulars of their lives.

"You are too young to help anybody and I am too old," he said. "By help I don't mean a courtesy like serving chokecherry jelly or giving money.

"Help," he said, "is giving part of yourself to somebody who comes to accept it willingly and needs it badly.

"So it is," he said, using an old homiletic transition, "that we can seldom help anybody. Either we don't know what part to give or maybe we don't like to give any part of ourselves. Then, more often than not, the part that is needed is not wanted. And even more often, we do not have the part that is needed. It is like the auto-supply shop over town where they always say, 'Sorry, we are just out of that part.'"

I told him, "You make it too tough. Help doesn't have to be anything that big."

He asked me, "Do you think your mother helps him by buttering his rolls?"

"She might," I told him. "In fact, yes, I think she does."

"Do you think you help him?" he asked me.

"I try to," I said. "My trouble is I don't know him. In fact, one of my troubles is that I don't even know whether he needs help. I don't know, that's my trouble."

"That should have been my text," my father said. "We are willing to help, Lord, but what if anything is needed?

"I still know how to fish," he concluded. "Tomorrow we will go fishing with him."

I lay waiting a long time before finally falling asleep. I felt the rest of the upstairs was also waiting.

Usually, I get up early to observe the commandment observed by only some of us—to arise early to see as much of the Lord's daylight as is given to us. I several times heard my brother open my door, study my covers, and then close my door. I began waking up by remembering that my brother, no matter what, was never late for work or fishing. One step closer to waking and I remembered that this was the trip when my brother was taking care of me. Now it began to seep into me that he was making my breakfast, and, when this became a matter of knowledge, I got up and dressed. All three were sitting at the table, drinking tea and waiting.

Mother said, as if she had wakened to find herself Queen for a Day, "Paul made breakfast for us." This made him feel good enough to smile early in the morning, but when he was serving me I looked closely and could see the blood vessels in his eyes. A fisherman, though, takes a hangover as a matter of course—after a couple of hours of fishing, it goes away, all except the dehydration, but then he is standing all day in water.

We somehow couldn't get started that morning. After Paul and I had left home, Father put away his fishing tackle, probably thinking he was putting it away for good, so now he couldn't remember where. Mother had to find most of the things for him. She knew nothing about fishing or fishing tackle, but she knew how to find things, even when she did not know what they looked like.

Paul, who usually got everyone nervous by being impatient to be on the stream, kept telling Father, "Take it easy. It's turned cooler. We'll make a killing today. Take it easy." But my father, from whom my brother had inherited his impatience to have his flies on water, would look at me visibly loathing himself for being old and not able to collect himself.

My mother had to go from basement to attic and to most closets in between looking for a fishing basket while she made lunches for three men, each of whom wanted a different kind of sandwich. After she got us in the car, she checked each car door to see that none of her men would fall out. Then she dried her hands in her apron, although her hands were not wet, and said, "Thank goodness," as we drove away.

I was at the wheel, and I knew before we started just where we were going. It couldn't be far up the Blackfoot, because we were starting late, and it had to be a stretch of water of two or three deep holes for Paul and me and one good hole with no bank too steep for Father to crawl down. Also, since he couldn't wade, the good fishing water had to be on his side of the river. They argued while I drove, although they knew just as well as I did where we had to go, but each one in our family considered himself the leading authority on how to fish the Blackfoot River. When we came to the side road going to the river above the mouth of Belmont Creek, they spoke in unison for the first time. "Turn here," they said, and, as if I were following their directions, I turned to where I was going anyway.

The side road brought us down to a flat covered with ground boulders and cheat grass. No livestock grazed on it, and grasshoppers took off like birds and flew great distances, because on this flat it is a long way between feeding grounds, even for grasshoppers. The flat itself and its crop of boulders are the roughly ground remains of one of geology's great disasters. The flat may well have been the end of the ice age lake, half as big as Lake Michigan, that in places was two thousand feet deep until the glacial dam broke and this hydraulic monster of the hills charged out on to the plains of eastern Washington. High on the mountains above where we stopped to fish are horizontal scars slashed by passing icebergs.

I had to be careful driving toward the river so I wouldn't high-center the car on a boulder and break the crankcase. The flat ended suddenly and the river was down a steep bank, blinking silver through the trees and then turning to blue by comparing itself to a red and green cliff. It was another world to see and feel, and another world of rocks. The boulders on the flat were shaped by the last ice age only eighteen or twenty thousand years ago, but the red and green precambrian rocks beside the blue water were almost from the basement of the world and time.

We stopped and peered down the bank. I asked my father, "Do you remember when we picked a lot of red and green rocks down there to build our fireplace? Some were red mudstones with ripples on them."

"Some had raindrops on them," he said. His imagination was always stirred by the thought that he was standing in ancient rain spattering on mud before it became rocks.

"Nearly a billion years ago," I said, knowing what he was thinking.

He paused. He had given up the belief that God had created all there was, including the Blackfoot River, on a six-day work schedule, but he didn't believe that the job so taxed God's powers that it took Him forever to complete.

"Nearly *half* a billion years ago," he said as his contribution to reconciling science and religion. He hurried on, not wishing to waste any part of old age in debate, except over fishing. "We carried those big rocks up the bank," he said, "but now I can't crawl down it. Two holes below, though, the river comes out in the open and there is almost no bank. I'll walk down there and fish, and you fish the first two holes. I'll wait in the sun. Don't hurry."

Paul said, "You'll get 'em," and all of a sudden Father was confident in himself again. Then he was gone.

We could catch glimpses of him walking along the bank of the river which had been the bottom of the great glacial lake. He held his rod straight in front of him and every now and then he lunged forward with it, perhaps reenacting some glacial race memory in which he speared a hairy ice age mastodon and ate him for breakfast.

Paul said, "Let's fish together today." I knew then that he was still taking care of me, because we almost always split up when we fished. "That's fine," I said. "I'll wade across and fish the other side," he said. I said, "Fine," again, and was doubly touched. On the other side you were backed against cliffs and trees, so it was mostly a roll-casting job, never my specialty. Besides, the river was powerful here with no good place to wade, and next to fishing Paul liked swimming rivers with his rod in his hand. It turned out he didn't have to swim here, but as he waded sometimes the wall of water rose to his upstream shoulder while it would be no higher than his hip behind him. He stumbled to shore from the weight of water in his clothes, and gave me a big wave.

I came down the bank to catch fish. Cool wind had blown in from Canada without causing any electric storms, so the fish should be off the bottom and feeding again. When a deer comes to water, his head shoots in and out of his shoulders to see what's ahead, and I was looking all around to see what fly to put on. But I didn't have to look further than my neck or my nose. Big clumsy flies bumped into my face, swarmed on my neck and wiggled in my underwear. Blundering and soft-bellied, they had been born before they had brains. They had spent a year under water on legs, had crawled out on a rock, had become flies and copulated with the ninth and tenth segments of their abdomens, and then had died as the first light wind blew them into the water where the fish circled excitedly. They were a fish's dream come true— stupid, succulent, and exhausted from copulation. Still, it would be hard to know what gigantic portion of human life is spent in this same ratio of years under water on legs to one premature, exhausted moment on wings.

I sat on a log and opened my fly box. I knew I had to get a fly that would match these flies exactly, because when a big hatch like this or the salmon fly is out, the fish won't touch anything else. As proof, Paul hadn't had a strike yet, so far as I could see.

I figured he wouldn't have the right fly, and I knew I

had it. As I explained earlier, he carried all his flies in his hat-band. He thought that with four or five generals in different sizes he could imitate the action of nearly any aquatic or terrestrial insect in any stage from larval to winged. He was always kidding me because I carried so many flies. "My, my," he would say, peering into my fly box, "wouldn't it be wonderful if a guy knew how to use ten of all those flies." But I've already told you about the Bee, and I'm still sure that there are times when a general won't turn a fish over. The fly that would work now had to be a big fly, it had to have a yellow, black-banded body, and it had to ride high in the water with extended wings, something like a butterfly that has had an accident and can't dry its wings by fluttering in the water.

It was so big and flashy it was the first fly I saw when I opened my box. It was called a Bunyan Bug, tied by a fly tyer in Missoula named Norman Means, who ties a line of big flashy flies all called Bunyan Bugs. They are tied on big hooks, No. 2's and No. 4's, have cork bodies with stiff horsehair tied crosswise so they ride high in the water like dragonflies on their backs. The cork bodies are painted different colors and then are shellacked. Probably the biggest and flashiest of the hundred flies my brother made fun of was the Bunyan Bug No. 2 Yellow Stone Fly.

I took one look at it and felt perfect. My wife, my mother-in-law, and my sister-in-law, each in her somewhat obscure style, had recently redeclared their love for me. I, in my somewhat obscure style, had returned their love. I might never see my brother-in-law again. My mother had found my father's old tackle and once more he was fishing with us. My brother was taking tender care of me, and not catching any fish. I was about to make a killing.

It is hard to cast Bunyan Bugs into the wind because the cork and horsehair make them light for their bulk. But, though the wind shortens the cast, it acts at the same time to lower the fly slowly and almost vertically to the water with no telltale splash. My Stone Fly was still hanging over the water when what seemed like a speed-boat went by it, knocked it high into the air, circled, opened the throttle wide on the returning straight away, and roared over the spot marked X where the Stone Fly had settled. Then the speedboat turned into a submarine, disappearing with all on board including my fly, and headed for deep water. I couldn't throw line into the rod fast enough to keep up with what was disappearing and I couldn't change its course. Not being as fast as what was under water, I literally forced it into the air. From where I was I suppose I couldn't see what happened, but my heart was at the end of the line and telegraphed back its impressions as it went by. My general impression was that marine life had turned into a rodeo. My particular information was that a large Rainbow had gone sun-fishing, turning over twice in the air, hitting my line each time and tearing loose from the fly which went sailing out into space. My distinct information was that it never looked around to see. My only close-at-hand information was that when the line was reeled in, there was nothing on the end of it but some cork and some hairs from a horse's tail.

The stone flies were just as thick as ever, fish still swirled in quiet water, and I was a little smarter. I don't care much about taking instructions, even from myself, but before I made the next cast I underlined the fact that big Rainbows sometimes come into quiet waters because aquatic insects hatch in or near quiet waters. "Be prepared," I said to myself, remembering an old war song. I also accepted my own advice to have some extra coils of line in my left hand to take some of the tension off the first run of the next big Rainbow swirling in quiet water.

So on this wonderful afternoon when all things came together it took me one cast, one fish, and some reluctantly accepted advice to attain perfection. I did not miss another.

From then on I let them run so far that sometimes they surged clear across the river and jumped right in front of Paul.

When I was young, a teacher had forbidden me to say "more perfect" because she said if a thing is perfect it can't be more so. But by now I had seen enough of life to have regained my confidence in it. Twenty minutes ago I had felt perfect, but by now my brother was taking off his hat and changing flies every few casts. I knew he didn't carry any such special as a Bunyan Bug No. 2 Yellow Stone Fly. I had five or six big Rainbows in my basket which began to hurt my shoulder so I left it behind on shore. Once in a while I looked back and smiled at the basket. I could hear it thumping on the rocks and falling on its side. However I may have violated grammar, I was feeling more perfect with every Rainbow.

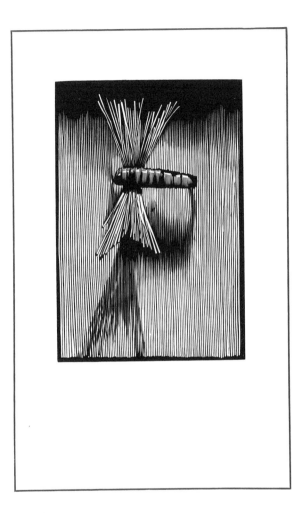

Bunyan Bug Yellow Stone Fly

Tied by Norman Means.

Just after my basket gave an extra large thump there was an enormous splash in the water to the left of where I was casting. "My God," I thought before I could look, "there's nothing that big that swims in the Blackfoot," and, when I dared look, there was nothing but a large circle that got bigger and bigger. Finally the first wave went by my knees. "It must be a beaver," I thought. I was waiting for him to surface when something splashed behind me. "My God," I said again, "I would have seen a beaver swim by me under water." While I was wrenching my neck backwards, the thing splashed right in front of me, too close for comfort but close enough so I could watch what was happening under water. The silt was rising from the bottom like smoke from the spot where lightning had struck. A fair-sized rock was sitting in the spot where the smoke was rising.

While I was relating my past to the present rock, there was another big splash in front of me, but this time I didn't bother to jump.

Beaver, hell! Without looking, I knew it was my brother. It didn't happen often in this life, only when his fishing partner was catching fish and he couldn't. It was a sight, however rare, that he could not bear to watch. So he would spoil his partner's hole, even if it was his brother's. I looked up just in time to see a fair-sized boulder come out of the sky and I ducked to late to keep it from splashing all over me.

He had his hat off and he shook his fist at me. I knew he had fished around his hat band before he threw the rocks. I shook my fist back at him, and waded to shore, where my basket was still thumping. In all my life, I had got the rock treatment only a couple of times before. I was feeling more perfect than ever.

I didn't mind that he spoiled the hole before I had filled my basket, because there was another big hole between us and father. It was a beautiful stretch of water, against cliffs and in shadows. The hole I had just fished was mostly in sunlight—the weather had become cooler, but was still warm enough so that the hole ahead in shadows should be even better than the one in sunlight and I should have no trouble finishing off my basket with a Bunyan Bug No. 2 Yellow Stone Fly.

Paul and I walked nearly the length of the first hole before we could hear each other yell across the river. I knew he hated to be heard yelling, "What were they biting on?" The last two words, "biting on," kept echoing across the water and pleased me.

When the echoes ceased, I yelled back, "Yellow stone flies." These words kept saying themselves until they subsided into sounds of the river. He kept turning his hat round and round in his hands.

I possibly began to get a little ashamed of myself. "I caught them on a Bunyan Bug," I yelled. "Do you want one?"

"No," he yelled before "want one" had time to echo. Then "want one" and "no" passed each other on the back turns.

"I'll wade across with one," I said through the cup of my hands. That's a lot to say across a river, and the first part of it returning met the last part of it just starting. I didn't know whether he had understood what I had said, but the river still answered, "No."

While I was standing in quiet, shady water, I half noticed that no stone flies were hatching, and I should have thought longer about what I saw but instead I found myself thinking about character. It seems somehow natural to start thinking about character when you get ahead of somebody, especially about the character of the one who is behind. I was thinking of how, when things got tough, my brother looked to himself to get himself out of trouble. He never looked for any flies from me. I had a whole round of thoughts on this subject before I returned to reality and yellow stone flies. I started by thinking that, though he was my brother, he was sometimes knot-headed. I pursued this line of thought back to the Greeks who believed that not wanting any help might even get you killed. Then I suddenly remembered that my brother was almost always a winner and often because he didn't borrow flies. So I decided that the response we make to character on any given day depends largely on the response fish are making to character on the same day. And thinking of the response of fish, I shifted rapidly back to reality, and said to myself, "I still have one more hole to go."

I didn't get a strike and I didn't see a stone fly and it was the same river as the one above, where I could have caught my limit a few minutes before if my brother hadn't thrown rocks in it. My prize Bunyan Bug began to look like a fake to me as well as to the fish. To me, it looked like a floating mattress. I cast it upstream and let it drift down naturally as if it had died. Then I popped it into the water as if it had been blown there. Then I made it zigzag while retrieving it, as if it were trying to launch itself into flight. But it evidently retained the appearance of a floating mattress. I took it off, and tried several other flies. There were no flies in the water for me to match, and by the same token there were no fish jumping.

I began to cast glances across the river under my hat brim. Paul wasn't doing much either. I saw him catch one, and he just turned and walked to shore with it, so it couldn't have been much of a fish. I was feeling a little less than more perfect.

Then Paul started doing something he practically never did, at least not since he had been old enough to be cocky. He suddenly started fishing upstream, back over the water he had just fished. That's more like me when I feel I haven't fished the hole right or from the right angle, but, when my brother fished a hole, he assumed nothing was left behind that could be induced to change its mind.

I was so startled I leaned against a big rock to watch.

Almost immediately he started hauling them in. Big ones, and he didn't spend much time landing them either. I thought he gave them too little line and took them in too fast, but I knew what he was up to. He expected to make a killing in this hole, and he wasn't going to let any one fish thrash around in the water until it scared the rest off. He had one on now and he held the line on it so tight he was forcing it high in the air. When it jumped, he leaned back on his rod and knocked the fish into the water again. Full of air now, it streaked across the top of the water with its tail like the propeller of a seaplane until it could get its submarine chambers adjusted and submerge again.

He lost a couple but he must have had ten by the time he got back to the head of the hole.

Then he looked across the river and saw me sitting beside my rod. He started fishing again, stopped, and took another look. He cupped his hands and yelled, "Do you have George's No. 2 Yellow Hackle with a feather not a horsehair wing?" It was fast water and I didn't get all the words immediately. "No. 2" I caught first, because it is a hell of a big hook, and then "George," because he was our fishing pal, and then "Yellow." With that much information I started to look in my box, and let the other words settle into a sentence later.

One bad thing about carrying a box loaded with flies, as I do, is that nearly half the time I still don't have the right one.

"No," I admitted across the water, and water keeps repeating your admissions.

"I'll be there," he called back and waded upstream.

"No," I yelled after him, meaning don't stop fishing on my account. You can't convey an implied meaning across a river, or, if you can, it is easy to ignore. My brother walked to the lower end of the first hole where the water was shallow and waded across.

By the time he got to me, I had recovered most of the pieces he must have used to figure out what the fish were biting. From the moment he had started fishing upstream his rod was at such a slant and there was so much slack in his line that he must have been fishing with a wet fly and letting it sink. In fact, the slack was such that he must have been letting the fly sink five or six inches. So when I was fishing this hole as I did the last one—with a cork-body fly that rides on top of the water—I was fighting the last war. "No. 2" hook told me of course it was a hell of a big insect, but "yellow" could mean a lot of things. My big question by the time he got to me was, "Are they biting on some aquatic insect in a larval or nymph stage or are they biting on a drowned fly?"

He gave me a pat on the back and one of George's No. 2 Yellow Hackles with a feather wing. He said, "They are feeding on drowned yellow stone flies."

I asked him, "How did you think that out?"

He thought back on what had happened like a reporter. He started to answer, shook his head when he found he was wrong, and then started out again. "All there is to thinking," he said, "is seeing something noticeable which makes you see something you weren't noticing which makes you see something that isn't even visible."

I said to my brother, "Give me a cigarette and say what you mean."

"Well," he said, "the first thing I noticed about this hole was that my brother wasn't catching any. There's nothing more noticeable to a fisherman than that his partner isn't catching any.

"This made me see that I hadn't seen any stone flies flying around this hole."

Then he asked me, "What's more obvious on earth than sunshine and shadow, but until I really saw that there were no stone flies hatching here I didn't notice that the upper hole where they were hatching was mostly in sunshine and this hole was in shadow."

I was thirsty to start with, and the cigarette made my mouth drier so I flipped the cigarette into the water.

"Then I knew," he said, "if there were flies in this hole they had to come from the hole above that's in the sunlight where there's enough heat to make them hatch.

"After that, I should have seen them dead in the water. Since I couldn't see them dead in the water, I knew they had to be at least six or seven inches under the water where I couldn't see them. So that's where I fished."

He leaned against a big rock with his hands behind his head to make the rock soft. "Wade out there and try George's No. 2," he said, pointing at the fly he had given me.

I didn't catch one right away, and I didn't expect to. My side of the river was the quiet water, the right side to be on in the hole above where the stone flies were hatching, but the drowned stone flies were washed down in the powerful water on the other side of this hole. After seven or eight casts, though, a small ring appeared on the surface. A small ring usually means that a small fish has risen to the surface, but it can also mean a big fish has rolled under water. If it is a big fish under water, he won't look so much like a fish as an arch of a rainbow that has appeared and disappeared.

Paul didn't even wait to see if I landed him. He waded out to talk to me. He went on talking as if I had time to listen to him and land a big fish. He said, "I'm going to wade back again and fish the rest of the hole." Sometimes I said, "Yes," and when the fish went out of the water, speech failed me, and when the fish made a long run I said at the end of it, "You'll have to say that over again."

Finally, we understood each other. He was going to wade the river again and fish the other side. We both should fish fairly fast, because Father probably was already waiting for us. Paul threw his cigarette in the water and was gone without seeing whether I landed the fish.

Not only was I on the wrong side of the river to fish with drowned stone flies, but Paul was a good enough roll caster to have already fished most of my side from his own. But I caught two more. They also started as little circles that looked like little fish feeding on the surface but were broken arches of big rainbows under water. After I caught these two, I quit. They made ten, and the last three were the finest fish I ever caught. They weren't the biggest or most spectacular fish I ever caught, but they were three fish I caught because my brother waded across the river to give me the fly that would catch them and because they were the last fish I ever caught fishing with him.

After cleaning my fish, I set these three apart with a layer of grass and wild mint.

Then I lifted the heavy basket, shook myself into the shoulder strap until it didn't cut any more, and thought, "I'm through for the day. I'll go down and sit on the bank by my father and talk." Then I added, "If he doesn't feel like talking, I'll just sit."

I could see the sun ahead. The coming burst of light made it look from the shadows that I and a river inside the earth were about to appear on earth. Although I could as 147 yet see only the sunlight and not anything in it, I knew my father was sitting somewhere on the bank. I knew partly because he and I shared many of the same impulses, even to quitting at about the same time. I was sure without as yet being able to see into what was in front of me that he was sitting somewhere in the sunshine reading the New Testament in Greek. I knew this both from instinct and experience.

Old age had brought him moments of complete peace. Even when we went duck hunting and the roar of the early morning shooting was over, he would sit in the blind wrapped in an old army blanket with his Greek New Testament in one hand and his shotgun in the other. When a stray duck happened by, he would drop the book and raise the gun, and, after the shooting was over, he would raise the book again, occasionally interrupting his reading to thank his dog for retrieving the duck.

The voices of the subterranean river in the shadows were different from the voices of the sunlit river ahead. In the shadows against the cliff the river was deep and engaged in profundities, circling back on itself now and then to say things over to be sure it had understood itself. But the river ahead came out into the sunny world like a chatterbox, doing its best to be friendly. It bowed to one shore and then to the other so nothing would feel neglected.

By now I could see inside the sunshine and had located

my father. He was sitting high on the bank. He wore no hat. Inside the sunlight, his faded red hair was once again ablaze and again in glory. He was reading, although evidently only by sentences because he often looked away from the book. He did not close the book until some time after he saw me.

I scrambled up the bank and asked him, "How many did you get?" He said, "I got all I want." I said, "But how many did you get?" He said, "I got four or five." I asked, "Are they any good?" He said, "They are beautiful."

He was about the only man I ever knew who used the word "beautiful" as a natural form of speech, and I guess I picked up the habit from hanging around him when I was little.

"How many did you catch?" he asked. "I also caught all I want," I told him. He omitted asking me just how many that was, but he did ask me, "Are they any good?" "They are beautiful," I told him, and sat down beside him.

"What have you been reading?" I asked. "A book," he said. It was on the ground on the other side of him. So I would not have to bother to look over his knees to see it, he said, "A good book."

Then he told me, "In the part I was reading it says the Word was in the beginning, and that's right. I used to think water was first, but if you listen carefully you will hear that the words are underneath the water."

"That's because you are a preacher first and then a fisherman," I told him. "If you ask Paul, he will tell you that the words are formed out of water."

"No," my father said, "you are not listening carefully.

Norman Maclean

The water runs over the words. Paul will tell you the same thing. Where is Paul anyway?"

I told him he had gone back to fish the first hole over again. "But he promised to be here soon," I assured him. "He'll be here when he catches his limit," he said. "He'll be here soon," I reassured him, partly because I could already see him in the subterranean shadows.

My father went back to reading and I tried to check what we had said by listening. Paul was fishing fast, picking up one here and there and wasting no time in walking them to shore. When he got directly across from us, he held up a finger on each hand and my father said, "He needs two more for his limit."

I looked to see where the book was left open and knew just enough Greek to recognize *Λογος* as the Word. I guessed from it and the argument that I was looking at the first verse of John. While I was looking, Father said, "He has one on."

It was hard to believe, because he was fishing in front of us on the other side of the hole that Father had just fished. Father slowly rose, found a good-sized rock and held it behind his back. Paul landed the fish, and waded out again for number twenty and his limit. Just as he was making the first cast, Father threw the rock. He was old enough so that he threw awkwardly and afterward had to rub his shoulder, but the rock landed in the river about where Paul's fly landed and at about the same time, so you can see where my brother learned to throw rocks into his partner's fishing water when he couldn't bear to see his partner catch any more fish.

Paul was startled for only a moment. Then he spotted Father on the bank rubbing his shoulder, and Paul laughed, shook his fist at him, backed to shore and went downstream until he was out of rock range. From there he waded into the water and began to cast again, but now he was far enough away so we couldn't see his line or loops. He was a man with a wand in a river, and whatever happened we had to guess from what the man and the wand and the river did.

As he waded out, his big right arm swung back and forth. Each circle of his arm inflated his chest. Each circle was faster and higher and longer until his arm became defiant and his chest breasted the sky. On shore we were sure, although we could see no line, that the air above him was singing with loops of line that never touched the water but got bigger and bigger each time they passed and sang. And we knew what was in his mind from the lengthening defiance of his arm. He was not going to let his fly touch any water close to shore where the small and middle-sized fish were. We knew from his arm and chest that all parts of him were saying, "No small one for the last one." Everything was going into one big cast for one last big fish.

From our angle high on the bank, my father and I could see where in the distance the wand was going to let the fly first touch water. In the middle of the river was a rock iceberg, just its tip exposed above water and underneath it a rock house. It met all the residential requirements for big fish—powerful water carrying food to the front and back doors, and rest and shade behind them.

My father said, "There has to be a big one out there."

I said, "A little one couldn't live out there."

My father said, "The big one wouldn't let it."

My father could tell by the width of Paul's chest that he was going to let the next loop sail. It couldn't get any wider. "I wanted to fish out there," he said, "but I couldn't cast that far."

Paul's body pivoted as if he were going to drive a golf ball three hundred yards, and his arm went high into the great arc and the tip of his wand bent like a spring, and then everything sprang and sang.

Suddenly, there was an end of action. The man was immobile. There was no bend, no power in the wand. It pointed at ten o'clock and ten o'clock pointed at the rock. For a moment the man looked like a teacher with a pointer illustrating something about a rock to a rock. Only water moved. Somewhere above the top of the rock house a fly was swept in water so powerful only a big fish could be there to see it.

Then the universe stepped on its third rail. The wand jumped convulsively as it made contact with the magic current of the world. The wand tried to jump out of the man's right hand. His left hand seemed to be frantically waving goodbye to a fish, but actually was trying to throw enough line into the rod to reduce the voltage and ease the shock of what had struck.

Everything seemed electrically charged but electrically unconnected. Electrical sparks appeared here and there on the river. A fish jumped so far downstream that it seemed outside the man's electrical field, but, when the fish had jumped, the man had leaned back on the rod and it was then that the fish had toppled back into the water not guided in its reentry by itself. The connections between the convulsions and the sparks became clearer by repetition. When the man leaned back on the wand and the fish reentered the water not altogether under its own power, the wand recharged with convulsions, the man's hand waved frantically at another departure, and much farther below a fish jumped again. Because of the connections, it became the same fish.

The fish made three such long runs before another act in the performance began. Although the act involved a big man and a big fish, it looked more like children playing. The man's left hand sneakily began recapturing line, and then, as if caught in the act, threw it all back into the rod as the fish got wise and made still another run.

"He'll get him," I assured my father.

"Beyond doubt," my father said. The line going out became shorter than what the left hand took in.

When Paul peered into the water behind him, we knew he was going to start working the fish to shore and didn't want to back into a hole or rock. We could tell he had worked the fish into shallow water because he held the rod higher and higher to keep the fish from bumping into anything on the bottom. Just when we thought the performance was over, the wand convulsed and the man thrashed through the water after some unseen power departing for the deep.

"The son of a bitch still has fight in him," I thought I said to myself, but unmistakably I said it out loud, and was embarrassed for having said it out loud in front of my father. He said nothing.

Two or three more times Paul worked him close to shore, only to have him swirl and return to the deep, but even at that distance my father and I could feel the ebbing of the underwater power. The rod went high in the air, and the man moved backwards swiftly but evenly, motions which when translated into events meant the fish had tried to rest for a moment on top of the water and the man had quickly raised the rod high and skidded him to shore before the fish thought of getting under water again. He skidded him across the rocks clear back to a sandbar before the shocked fish gasped and discovered he could not live in oxygen. In belated despair, he rose in the sand and consumed the rest of momentary life dancing the Dance of Death on his tail.

The man put the wand down, got on his hands and knees in the sand, and, like an animal, circled another animal and waited. Then the shoulder shot straight out, and my brother stood up, faced us, and, with uplifted arm proclaimed himself the victor. Something giant dangled from his fist. Had Romans been watching they would have thought that what was dangling had a helmet on it.

"That's his limit," I said to my father.

"He is beautiful," my father said, although my brother had just finished catching his limit in the hole my father had already fished.

This was the last fish we were ever to see Paul catch. My father and I talked about this moment several times later, and whatever our other feelings, we always felt it fitting that, when we saw him catch his last fish, we never saw the fish but only the artistry of the fisherman.

While my father was watching my brother, he reached over to pat me, but he missed, so he had to turn his eyes and look for my knee and try again. He must have thought that I felt neglected and that he should tell me he was proud of me also but for other reasons.

It was a little too deep and fast where Paul was trying to wade the river, and he knew it. He was crouched over the water and his arms were spread wide for balance. If you were a wader of big rivers you could have felt with him even at a distance the power of the water making his legs weak and wavy and ready to swim out from under him. He looked downstream to estimate how far it was to an easier place to wade.

My father said, "He won't take the trouble to walk downstream. He'll swim it." At the same time Paul thought the same thing, and put his cigarettes and matches in his hat.

My father and I sat on the bank and laughed at each other. It never occurred to either of us to hurry to the shore in case he needed help with a rod in his right hand and a basket loaded with fish on his left shoulder. In our family it was no great thing for a fisherman to swim a river with matches in his hair. We laughed at each other because we knew he was getting damn good and wet, and we lived in him, and were swept over the rocks with him and held his rod high in one of our hands.

As he moved to shore he caught himself on his feet and then was washed off them, and, when he stood again, more of him showed and he staggered to shore. He never stopped to shake himself. He came charging up the bank showering molecules of water and images of himself to show what was sticking out of his basket, and he dripped all over us, like a young duck dog that in its joy forgets to shake itself before getting close.

"Let's put them all out on the grass and take a picture of them," he said. So we emptied our baskets and arranged them by size and took turns photographing each other admiring them and ourselves. The photographs turned out to be like most amateur snapshots of fishing catches—the fish were white from overexposure and didn't look as big as they actually were and the fishermen looked self-conscious as if some guide had to catch the fish for them.

However, one closeup picture of him at the end of this day remains in my mind, as if fixed by some chemical bath. Usually, just after he finished fishing he had little to say unless he saw he could have fished better. Otherwise, he merely smiled. Now flies danced around his hatband. Large drops of water ran from under his hat on to his face and then into his lips when he smiled.

At the end of this day, then, I remember him both as a distant abstraction in artistry and as a closeup in water and laughter.

My father always felt shy when compelled to praise one of his family, and his family always felt shy when he praised them. My father said, "You are a fine fisherman."

My brother said, "I'm pretty good with a rod, but I need three more years before I can think like a fish."

Remembering that he had caught his limit by switching to George's No. 2 Yellow Hackle with a feather wing,

I said without knowing how much I said, "You already know how to think like a dead stone fly."

We sat on the bank and the river went by. As always, it was making sounds to itself, and now it made sounds to us. It would be hard to find three men sitting side by side who knew better what a river was saying.

On the Big Blackfoot River above the mouth of Belmont Creek the banks are fringed by large Ponderosa pines. In the slanting sun of late afternoon the shadows of great branches reached from across the river, and the trees took the river in their arms. The shadows continued up the bank, until they included us.

A river, though, has so many things to say that it is hard to know what it says to each of us. As we were packing our tackle and fish in the car, Paul repeated, "Just give me three more years." At the time, I was surprised at the repetition, but later I realized that the river somewhere, sometime, must have told me, too, that he would receive no such gift. For, when the police sergeant early next May wakened me before daybreak, I rose and asked no questions. Together we drove across the Continental Divide and down the length of the Big Blackfoot River over forest floors yellow and sometimes white with glacier lilies to tell my father and mother that my brother had been beaten to death by the butt of a revolver and his body dumped in an alley.

My mother turned and went to her bedroom where, in a house full of men and rods and rifles, she had faced most of her great problems alone. She was never to ask me a question about the man she loved most and understood least. Perhaps she knew enough to know that for her it was enough to have loved him. He was probably the only man in the world who had held her in his arms and leaned back and laughed.

When I finished talking to my father, he asked, "Is there anything else you can tell me?"

Finally, I said, "Nearly all the bones in his hand were broken."

He almost reached the door and then turned back for reassurance. "Are you sure that the bones in his hand were broken?" he asked. I repeated, "Nearly all the bones in his hand were broken." "In which hand?" he asked. "In his right hand," I answered.

After my brother's death, my father never walked very well again. He had to struggle to lift his feet, and, when he did get them up, they came down slightly out of control. From time to time Paul's right hand had to be reaffirmed; then my father would shuffle away again. He could not shuffle in a straight line from trying to lift his feet. Like many Scottish ministers before him, he had to derive what comfort he could from the faith that his son had died fighting.

For some time, though, he struggled for more to hold on to. "Are you sure you have told me everything you know about his death?" he asked. I said, "Everything." "It's not much, is it?" "No," I replied, "but you can love completely without complete understanding." "That I have known and preached," my father said.

Once my father came back with another question. "Do you think I could have helped him?" he asked. Even if I might have thought longer, I would have made the same answer. "Do you think I could have helped him?" I answered. We stood waiting in deference to each other. How can a question be answered that asks a lifetime of questions?

After a long time he came with something he must have wanted to ask from the first. "Do you think it was just a stick-up and foolishly he tried to fight his way out? You know what I mean—that it wasn't connected with anything in his past."

"The police don't know," I said.

"But do you?" he asked, and I felt the implication.

"I've said I've told you all I know. If you push me far enough, all I really know is that he was a fine fisherman."

"You know more than that," my father said. "He was beautiful."

"Yes," I said, "he was beautiful. He should have been —you taught him."

My father looked at me for a long time—he just looked at me. So this was the last he and I ever said to each other about Paul's death.

Indirectly, though, he was present in many of our conversations. Once, for instance, my father asked me a series of questions that suddenly made me wonder whether I understood even my father whom I felt closer to than any man I have ever known. "You like to tell true stories, don't you?" he asked, and I answered, "Yes, I like to tell stories that are true."

Then he asked, "After you have finished your true

stories sometime, why don't you make up a story and the people to go with it?

"Only then will you understand what happened and why.

"It is those we live with and love and should know who elude us."

Now nearly all those I loved and did not understand when I was young are dead, but I still reach out to them.

Of course, now I am too old to be much of a fisherman, and now of course I usually fish the big waters alone, although some friends think I shouldn't. Like many fly fishermen in western Montana where the summer days are almost Arctic in length, I often do not start fishing until the cool of the evening. Then in the Arctic half-light of the canyon, all existence fades to a being with my soul and memories and the sounds of the Big Blackfoot River and a four-count rhythm and the hope that a fish will rise.

Eventually, all things merge into one, and a river runs through it. The river was cut by the world's great flood and runs over rocks from the basement of time. On some of the rocks are timeless raindrops. Under the rocks are the words, and some of the words are theirs.

I am haunted by waters.

This edition of *A River Runs Through It* was printed offset from the Pennyroyal Press edition, which was printed by letterpress at the Pennyroyal Press, West Hatfield, Massachusetts in the spring of 1989 by Harold P. McGrath. The staff of the press at the time of printing was Jeffrey P. Dwyer, Elizabeth O'Grady, and John Lancaster. The type is Monotype Van Dijck and was composed by Michael and Winifred Bixler at their foundry in Skaneateles, New York. The book was designed by Barry Moser who also drew and engraved the illustrations on end-grain boxwood blocks.

The project owes a very special debt of gratitude to George Croonenberghs, who tied all the flies depicted—and wrote the accompanying notes—with the exception of the "Bunyan Bug," which was tied by Norman Means. Gratitude is also expressed to Carroll Wilson, of the Hills Bros. Coffee Company, to Joel Snyder, and to Norman Maclean.